Blue Shirts

by

Michael Crisp

REMIX BOOKS

Published in Georgetown, KY

United States of America

Remix Books
PO Box 1303
Georgetown, KY 40324

www.Facebook.com/BlueShirtsBook

Layout and Cover Design
Kevin Kifer
www.k2-technology.com

ISBN 978-1-4951-3604-7

First Edition

Legal Disclaimer

dedication

To the reader:

"May you have as much fun reading this book as I had writing it."

One

The month of March is usually a very special time in Lexington, Kentucky, especially if you are a basketball fan. The city is home to the University of Kentucky Wildcats, which has been a college basketball powerhouse for as long as anyone can remember. Basketball is a year-round obsession here, but when "March Madness" arrives and the Wildcats begin play in the season-ending national tournament, it reaches a fever pitch. The entire city, as well as most of the state, drapes itself in blue and white as it cheers on the 'Cats. Although it is now March in Lexington, Kentucky, this isn't a story about basketball. It's a story about money, power, and sex.

Surprised? You shouldn't be. A story like this could happen in most anywhere across the country, it just so happens to take place in the bosom of the bluegrass state. Kentucky itself is a place that's full of secrets, some of which - like its coal and caves - are hidden underneath the ground, out of plain view. The darkest secrets, however, aren't buried beneath the earth. Instead, they rest within the hearts of the people who walk among us. People who we know, or at least think we know.

This story also involves one of Kentucky's most famous institutions - horse racing. Sure, the sport may not have been invented here, but it was certainly perfected here. After all, the Kentucky Derby takes place just 77 miles west of Lexington in the city of Louisville. Each year, on the first Saturday in May, the eyes of the world are upon Churchill Downs to behold the remarkable combination of power and beauty that is the thoroughbred race horse. As they circle the track, galloping against each other with blazing speed, it's easy to see why this event is called "the most exciting two minutes in sports."

This rare combination of power and beauty is not just reserved for the glorious creatures that are bolting down the track, but also for those who are watching the race in person. The grandstand is filled with thousands of people who are on hand to mix, mingle, wager and cheer. The men, dressed colorfully in their seersucker suits, talk loudly with each other as they chomp their cigars and gulp down their Mint Juleps. It's the women, however, who steal the show, with their stunning dresses and their large, flowery hats. One look into the gallery and it's clear that the Kentucky Derby is just as much of a social event than a sporting competition.

With its magnificent pomp and pageantry, the Kentucky Derby is the horse racing's signature event. Ironically, the journey to this legendary race often begins in the quiet countryside of central Kentucky. Yes, Lexington looms large across this landscape, but in the smaller towns that surround the city - towns with names like Versailles, Midway, Georgetown, Winchester, Nicholasville and Paris - this is where these dreams begin. Many of the world's most successful horse farms are located in these towns. The places are often large and opulent, and while taking a relaxing drive through the countryside, it's not uncommon to glance over the fence of one of these farms and see a multi-million dollar house situated next to a multi-million dollar barn. The houses are for living in, raising a family, and operating a business. The barns are where legends are born.

These farms come alive in the spring and summer, as the warm sun hovers over the lush, green grass, warming the leaves on the trees that are towering high above. But for now, that would have to wait, because it was March and the sun was nowhere to be seen. For weeks, the sky had been gray, the grass had been brown, and the trees were bare and scraggly.

This morning was a little different, however. It actually felt like the bitter cold of winter would soon be a distant memory, as the morning sun had finally emerged and begun to shine brightly, warming the downtown sidewalks and the people who were walking along them. A group of men dressed in suits were crossing the street, remarking how great it was to finally see the sun. A group of women were overheard talking about an upcoming weekend getaway at a nearby lake. There was also the usual frenzy of automobiles scurrying throughout the city, weaving in and out of traffic as they made their way into the parking lots and parking garages that were scattered throughout downtown. Among the vehicles was a black Chevrolet Suburban, glistening in the bright sun as it sped through the city. The SUV quickly changed lanes and darted quickly into a parking garage just a few minutes before 9 a.m.

Sean Everett closed the door of his Suburban. His dress shoes clicked loudly on the smooth concrete floor of the garage as he walked toward the elevator. As the doors opened, he entered the elevator, pushed the button for the 29th floor, and closed his eyes for a moment. When he opened them, he was staring at his reflection in the shiny steel doors. As the elevator began its ascent, he studied his reflection. He ran his hand through his wavy blonde hair, which he wore a bit long compared to other men in their early-forties. He was handsome, with dark brown eyes and an athletic build, which he liked to accentuate by wearing suits to work that were a little tighter than normal. He tightened his necktie, and pulled a piece of lint off of his rust-colored dress shirt as the elevator began to slow down. A bell chimed, and the doors opened.

Sean paused for a moment before exiting the elevator, running his hand across his stomach to smooth out a few wrinkles that he had just noticed in his shirt. As he stepped into the lobby, he was greeted by the receptionist, Kate, who was sitting behind her desk finishing up a phone call.

"Good morning, Sean," said the young brunette, with the familiar warm smile that he had grown accustomed to over the years.

Sean nodded, smiled and walked by her desk and into the small hallway that led to his office. As he sat at his desk, he tried to make himself comfortable. He poured a cup of coffee, glanced at the emails on his computer screen, and sorted through a few notes on his desk. Sean was a stockbroker, and this office had been like a home to him for the past twelve years as one of the top earners at Kenley & Logan, one of the city's most powerful brokerage firms. The company had been started in the 1970's by a couple of bankers from eastern Kentucky, and had recruited Sean when he was a young, up and-and-coming salesman for a securities firm across town. Just a few years ago he was considered the company's "rising star" - a born salesman who had an innate ability to connect with, and charm when necessary, the wealthiest men and women in the bluegrass state. He had a special connection with Lexington's older, society crowd, most of whom had inherited their wealth rather than earned it. Sean had brought many of these blue bloods into his office through the years, sold them on his ability to grow their portfolios, and add to their fortunes. He was very good at making his clients money, and through commissions, bonuses, and a sizeable salary, he had done well for himself.

Sean was still making a six-figure income, but the economy had taken a turn for the worse in recent years. He wasn't bringing in as much new business as he had in previous years, and mortality had claimed his wealthiest client, Dr. Frank Trammell, who passed away over the winter. Dr. Trammell was a quiet man in his early eighties, a retired physician who had purchased a great deal of commercial property in downtown Lexington in the 1970s. He was estranged from his children, all of whom Sean met at the reading of their father's will this past January. During that time, Dr. Trammell's eldest daughter let Sean know that they would be terminating their father's account with Kenley & Logan.

Finishing his coffee, Sean looked at the photograph in the picture frame on his desk, picked it up, and pulled it closer to him. He looked at the family within the frame - his wife of fifteen years, Jaclyn, his 12-year old son, Braden, and himself. The photograph of the smiling family used to automatically bring a smile to his face, but this time he was expressionless. Sean heard a tap on the wall and saw Kate standing in his doorway.

"David needs to see you," she said

"Okay," replied Sean, as he put the picture back on his desk and rose from his chair.

Sean walked back down the hallway, treading lightly on the light gray carpet that led into the office of David Logan. David was sitting behind his desk in the midst of a telephone conversation when he motioned for Sean to come in and have a seat. David, the son of one of the company founders, was Sean's boss. He was in his mid-fifties, dressed in a gray flannel business suit, and had commanded Kenley & Logan with a kindness that was rather uncommon in such a high-pressure industry. He wrapped up his phone call, rubbed his eyes with his fingers, and looked at Sean, who was seated across from him at the desk.

"Sean, we've been friends a long time," said David, "so long in fact that I consider you just as much of a friend as an employee."

Sean nodded, but remained silent.

"That's why it hurts me to tell you that we're letting you go," David said.

"You're laying me off?" Sean replied, with a confused expression on his face.

"Our business is down considerably," David continued, "and nobody is sure when the economy is going to straighten itself out. A lot of our older clients are divesting, and we're having a lot of trouble recruiting younger clients who are choosing to do their trading online. Unfortunately, we have to make a lot of painful business decisions going forward, and I'm afraid that this is just the first in a series of those decisions."

"I don't understand," Sean hastily replied. "I'm still making you money. Sure, it's been slow lately, but I still have clients that are making us money."

"It's not just you, Sean," countered David, "the whole industry is changing. Your clients, our clients - they're all getting older, and the next generation is investing their money differently. To tell you the truth, I don't know how much longer I can afford to keep the doors open here if it continues like it's been going."

"There must be something we can do," said Sean, as he leaned forward in his chair. "If you can just give me some time, I can figure this out."

"I wish I could," David replied, "especially considering your situation at home. Divorce isn't easy - hell, I've been through three of them so believe me - I know."

As David continued speaking, Sean's mind was elsewhere. He thought again of the picture of his family that was in his office. In his mind he could see Jaclyn, who had been his soul mate, his best friend, and most importantly, his wife of fifteen years. Earlier this week, however, their divorce was finalized. She was now officially his ex-wife, and it was something that he was still having trouble absorbing.

"Look Sean, you're young, and you're damn good at what you do," David said. "You'll find work soon, and more importantly, you'll bounce back from this whole divorce thing."

David stood up from his chair, slightly leaning over his desk. He extended his arm to shake Sean's hand. Sean paused, stood up from his chair, shook David's hand and left the room.

Two

Carrying a cardboard box under his arm, Sean exited the elevator and returned to the parking garage. He opened the passenger side door of his vehicle and placed the box, which contained the remnants of his last several years at the office - a couple of softball trophies, an unopened bottle of bourbon, an unopened pack of golf balls, and the framed photograph of his family.

He left downtown and made the 20-minute drive to his home, which was located on the edge of the county. As he approached the outskirts of the city, he began to realize that he was not only divorced, but he was jobless as well. His mind was racing as he hurried home along the curvy country roads that he navigated daily. He usually loved this drive and all of its scenery, with its horse farms, tobacco barns, old churches, and stacked stone fences, but today he hardly noticed anything except the road in front of him.

As he arrived at his house, he pulled into the long driveway, which wove its way up to his home like a long, concrete snake. It was a large, ranch-style home that sat atop a hill and overlooked five beautiful acres in the county. The bricks were dark brown, and looked almost reddish against the white trim of the windows that covered its exterior.

Rather than veering right towards his garage, he looked up to his left and saw Jaclyn's vehicle parked in the teardrop-shaped turnaround just outside his front door. Moments later, he watched as she maneuvered herself through the front door and on to the porch, balancing a laundry basket on her hip. As she moved carefully down the front steps, Sean parked behind her car and came up to her as she opened her trunk.

"This is the last of it," she said, then handed Sean her house key and placed the basket in the trunk of her car.

"Where's Braden?" asked Sean, hoping that their son was either inside the house or hiding in the car beneath a pile of clothes and shoes that filled her backseat.

"He's with my sister, she's off today. I didn't think it would be a good idea for him to be here anyway, you know, while I was moving the rest of my stuff out." Jaclyn paused for a moment. "You're home early for a Friday," she said, "Is everything okay?"

"I was laid off today," Sean replied.

"Oh, wow. I'm sorry to hear, Sean," responded Jaclyn. "What happened?"

"I'd rather not talk about it," he said. "But it looks like I'm going to need you to work with me on the child support payments for a while, if that's okay."

"I don't know if I can do that, Sean," she said in a voice that sounded both angry and concerned. "My first house payment is due in a few days, and Braden has a lot of expenses coming up next month too."

"Look, I just need some time to figure all of this out," replied Sean, raising his voice slightly as Jaclyn closed the trunk of her car. "This is all new to me - all of this."

"Just bring the check next week," Jaclyn said, "like you promised."

As he watched her car pull out of the driveway, Sean retrieved his box from his passenger seat of his truck, and sat on the steps of his front porch. He loosened his necktie and removed the bottle of bourbon from the box, opened it and took a drink. After swallowing the first gulp of whiskey, he again thought of Jaclyn - the tall, slender blonde who, as of this week, was no longer his spouse.

Even though she was now in her early forties, Jaclyn was still strikingly gorgeous and looked much younger than her age, especially when she wore blue jeans and her hair in a ponytail, which had come to be her signature look over the last few years. Originally from Corbin, a Kentucky town just a couple hours south of Lexington, her parents moved to central Kentucky when she was a child, purchasing a small horse farm in Versailles and turning it into one of the largest thoroughbred operations in the state. Jaclyn studied equine management at the University of Kentucky and hoped to take over their farm one day, but her parents were offered a staggering sum for the business and decided to sell it while she was in school. Her mother and father moved back to Corbin after the sale, which left Jaclyn heartbroken, so she left school and began selling real estate. Buoyed by her stunning looks and down-to-earth charm, she was successful from the onset. She got her start by selling starter homes during the housing boom of the 1990s, but after a few years in the business, her focus shifted to much larger homes, especially in Lexington's wealthiest subdivisions.

After a few months of dating, Sean and Jaclyn married in the summer of 1999. It was an elegant affair at Spindletop Hall, with the ceremony taking place on the lawn of the stately Lexington manor and the reception within the mansion itself. After a honeymoon cruise in the Carribean, the newlyweds settled into a newly-built home in the country. In 2002, they were blessed with a son, Braden, a handsome, blue-eyed blonde whose features heavily favored his mother.

Although their divorce was finalized a few days ago, their relationship had been disintegrating for months. At first, their arguments generally revolved around Sean's work, as he had been logging a lot more time at the office than usual. With the recent loss of some of his wealthier clients, he was picking up several smaller accounts to help maintain his income. Beginning in the fall, his hours at Kenley & Logan had increased dramatically, and by winter it seemed that he was hardly home at all. Jaclyn longed for more time with Sean, but he kept asking her to be patient - telling her that his load would be lighter once the economy improved. He promised that things would soon be different, and that the days of him spending a lot more time with her and Braden were "right around the corner" - a phrase that Jaclyn had grown tired of hearing.

After weeks of arguments, tempered with long periods of uncomfortable silence that lasted for days, Jaclyn told Sean that she was leaving him. She took Braden with her, and moved in with her sister. This took Sean by surprise, but he was so consumed with work that he couldn't focus on fixing his family. He was optimistic that Jaclyn would come back to him, and over dinner one night, there was a glimmer of hope. Jaclyn told Sean that she still loved him, and would come back home to him, but only if he left his job. She told him that his devotion to Kenley & Logan was driving a wedge in their marriage, and that she would help him find work elsewhere. Jaclyn didn't want to lose Sean, and she felt that a change of career would do him good. But Sean was obsessed with turning things around at the firm, and he was firmly against finding a new job. He refused to listen to Jaclyn, and a few days later, they began to work out the details of their divorce.

Sean wasn't a particularly emotional person, but the day after Jaclyn left home for good, he broke down and cried. It was a sobering moment for him, realizing that his relationship with her was over. He didn't like this feeling - this overwhelming helplessness that had shaken him to his very foundation. It was scary and overwhelming, and unlike anything he had ever experienced in his life. He searched inside himself of a way to deal with the pain, finally deciding that the best way to overcome it would be to make himself fall out of love with Jaclyn. And so he did. He blocked her from his thoughts, and tried his best to erase as many happy memories of her from his mind as possible, and focus instead on the painful memories. For the most part, he succeeded, and he was able to move on with his life the best way he knew how.

The breakup of the family was particularly hard on Braden, who broke down and cried when his father told him the news on the way back from a ski trip. To Sean, watching his son cry had been the hardest part of the divorce. At first, Braden had a lot of questions, and Sean did his best to answer them. At age 12, Braden's world was turning upside-down, and he was having a hard time adjusting to everything. He was close to his parents, and he had a special relationship with his father. Even though Sean hadn't been around the house much over the last few months, he had been overcompensating quite a bit lately, with ski trips, basketball games, and other activities that both men could enjoy together. Braden went through a cycle of emotions as he dealt with the divorce. He was sometimes detached, lost in his iPhone, iPad, and other assorted technologies, internalizing his emotions so he could handle the upheaval in his life. Other times he was cheerful and talkative, which would often lead to optimistic questions he would ask to both his parents regarding if there was a possibility that they would ever get back together.

When the custody arrangement was hammered out, it was decided that Sean would get Braden on Tuesdays and every other weekend. Sean was upset that his time would be so limited with his son, but he was used to it. After all, he had barely been home for the past several months, so this was nothing new. It was sad, but nothing new.

As he sat on his porch, taking the occasional swig from the bourbon bottle, Sean thought it was ironic that his overloaded work schedule had been the primary reason behind the demise of his marriage, and now his job, like his relationship with Jaclyn, was no more. He wondered if he still loved Jaclyn, and pondered if she would come back to him if he asked her. He remembered loving the woman that she was before the arguments began, but he realized that he wasn't in love with the woman that she had become. He missed the woman that he married, and questioned if that person still existed. For the last few months he had adopted some of Braden's methods for dealing with the divorce - a stoic façade, a calm demeanor, an internalization of everything that could bother or upset him. But now his emotions were coming to the surface, ranging from angry one minute to sad the next. He watched the afternoon sun begin to set on the horizon, sinking behind the old oak trees near the edge of his yard, and he realized that he had spent almost the entire day on his front porch. It was beginning to get colder when he decided to go inside, but then he heard a noise in the distance - it was a vehicle, and it was pulling into his driveway.

Three

It was certainly a strange sight - not just that the automobile approaching Sean's porch was a large sport-utility vehicle, but that it was a new, black Chevrolet Suburban, virtually identical to Sean's own truck. Because he was a little drunk, Sean briefly wondered if he was seeing double as the shiny black SUV pulled up behind his own truck and parked. As the engine shut off, the driver emerged and approached Sean, silhouetted somewhat by the fading sun.

"Sean Everett," said the man, with a slight laughter in his voice. "It's been a long time."

Sean hadn't heard that voice in years, and he was fairly certain whose voice it was. "Rob, is that you?" he asked, as he stood up to greet his friend.

"In the flesh, my man, in the flesh!" the dark-haired man replied.

The shadowy figure let out a huge laugh, trotted up the steps and hugged Sean, who invited him inside the house. Sean grabbed his bottle and his cardboard box, turned on the lights in the foyer, and the two men made their way to the kitchen. As his guest perched himself on a barstool next to the kitchen's island bar, Sean grabbed a couple of glasses from the cabinet, filled them with ice and bourbon, and sat down next to the man.

"It's been, what, sixteen years?" Sean inquired.

"More like seventeen, but who's counting," answered the man, whose laughter had now subsided to a simple smile.

The man was Rob Caldwell, an old friend of Sean's from what now seemed like ages ago.

Rob was a dashing man in his mid-forties, with short, jet black hair that was now peppered with a handful of silver streaks just over his temples. He was tall and tan, with deep blue eyes and a million-dollar smile. As he sat at the counter, Rob rolled up the sleeves of his dress shirt as Sean finished pouring the bourbon into his glass.

Sean had known Rob when they both attended high school, or better put, he had known of Rob. The two men weren't actually friends, and with Sean being three years younger than Rob, they didn't have any classes together or any other opportunities to interact with each other. But Rob, who was a senior when Sean was a freshman, was somewhat of a legendary figure to many of the other students in school. Rob was a boisterous, self-proclaimed "ladies man" who, despite the lack of any visible interaction with the opposite sex in or out of school, garnered the respect of Sean and many of his easily-impressed male classmates. Rob was always quick to brag about his most recent sexual conquest, or discuss the intimate details of a recent date with a classmate, but rarely were his stories ever verified. Sure, there were some who doubted Rob and his salacious stories, but the younger men in school were certain that he was telling the truth - mainly because they wanted what he said to be the truth. Like many of his friends at that age, Sean had girls on his mind constantly, and the world that Rob spoke of was filled with promise and possibility.

Sean immediately flashed back to high school, remembering when he encountered Rob for the first time. Sean was walking with his tray through the cafeteria when he saw Rob sitting at a table with a group of older boys. Rob was preaching loudly to the group of his classmates about his most prized "pickup" technique.

"Listen," Rob boasted loudly while pointing at his ear, as if he were conducting a seminar. "Women don't want you to talk - they want you to listen to them while they talk."

Sean took a seat at the adjoining table, and eavesdropped on the boisterous Rob as he continued to speak to the classmates that had gathered around him. As they cheered and nodded in agreement, Rob caught Sean, who was both curious and awestruck by the charismatic senior, staring at him. Rob then smiled at Sean, put his finger back up to his ear, smiled, and silently mouthed the word "listen", never breaking eye contact with the young student.

Sean's next experience with Rob came a few years later. Sean was 21, and he was attending the University of Kentucky. Most of his high school friends had moved away to study elsewhere, and he found himself spending most of his evenings at his dormitory on campus, waist deep in textbooks. Majoring in economics, he was an exceptional student, consistently making the dean's list by maintaining a 4.0 grade point average. He excelled in all of his classes, especially those involving accounting and mathematics.

Although the shy, skinny kid from high school had grown into a handsome young man, Sean was socially awkward and insecure. As his junior year came to a close, he began to realize that he spent three years in college but had barely developed any real relationships with any of his classmates. Although he was proud of his academic accomplishments as a student, Sean had become introverted, and was now somewhat of a "loner." His grades were beyond solid - they were spectacular - but that wasn't enough. He wanted a social life - friends, dating, perhaps even a girlfriend - the whole college experience. He didn't want to look back years from now and have regrets.

Sean had gone on a couple of dates during his sophomore year, mostly with girls who had nothing more than a passing interest in him. In his junior year, Sean developed a crush on a fellow classmate. Her name was Lily, who shared an English Literature class with Sean. Throughout the semester, he would sit two chairs behind her, admiring her long brown hair, soft voice and even softer features. He never found the courage to talk to Lily, who seemed quiet and shy herself. Sean devised a plan to remedy that one Friday afternoon while she was talking to another classmate. As she sat at her desk, Sean overheard her telling one of her girlfriends that she was struggling to finish writing a paper about William Shakespeare. Although his knowledge of Shakespeare was minimal at best, he wanted to impress the young woman by offering to help her with her assignment. Sean spent the weekend pouring through a vast array of poems and plays that Shakespeare had written, as well as reading a lengthy biography of the bard that he had found in the university's library. The following Monday, he felt confident enough to approach

Lily about helping her with her paper.

As he walked into the classroom, Sean saw Lily talking excitedly with the girlfriend she had been speaking with the week before. As he walked by the women to take his seat, he saw Lily extending her arm, showing off a diamond engagement ring to her friend. Lily gushed that she had received it over the weekend from her longtime boyfriend. Crushed, Sean walked between Lily and her friend, smiled politely, and took his seat.

Sean regressed for weeks after that, licking his wounds by throwing himself back into his studies. For a while it seemed like he might be destined to remain the quiet loner who spent most every day in class and most every night in his dorm room. Fortunately, that changed on the last day of his junior year. While sitting in his accounting class preparing to take his final exam, he overheard a couple of classmates talking about going out that evening to celebrate the end of the semester. One of the students, a preppie named Ben, noticed Sean listening to their conversation, so he invited Sean to join them. Sean jumped at the chance to accompany them. He had been pouring himself into his studies for so long that he was ready to pour beer into himself.

Later that night, Sean met up with the young men and women from his accounting class at a local watering hole for chicken wings and cheap draft beer. As the evening wore on, the girls in the group expressed their desire to go dancing. At first, the guys were opposed to spending the rest of the night at a dance club. They were perfectly content to remain where they were, as they were enjoying the quiet conversation, Budweisers and buffalo sauce. But the girls persisted, the men began to cave in a bit.

"Sean wants to go," exclaimed one of the girls, a pretty redhead named Kara. "You'll go dancing with us, won't you Sean?"

"Sure," answered Sean. "Why not? It sounds like fun."

Sean's response prompted groans from the rest of the young men, and proved to be the tipping point in the group's decision to leave the tavern. A few minutes later, Ben walked outside and hailed a taxi cab. The rest of the crew piled into the taxi, and Kara asked the driver to take them to The Speakeasy.

The Speakeasy was one of the few remaining dance clubs in the city. Getting its name from its 1920's gangster décor, the bar featured costumed employees, with bartenders garbed in zoot suits and cocktail waitresses dressed like flappers. The floors had a continuous, black and white checkerboard pattern, except for the dance floor, which was made of oak. The walls stretched nearly 20 feet high and featured detailed murals of legendary underworld characters like Al Capone and John Dillinger. In the 1950s, The Speakeasy had opened as a popular "supper club", featuring nationally-known musicians and a pricy menu. As the years changed, so did the club's format when their older clientele disappeared. Gone were the show bands and surf and turf dinners, replaced by a DJ and deep-fried appetizers. After a recession in the early 1970s, the club closed, and the ownership turned it into an upscale furniture store. But it reopened in the mid-1970s when disco music began sweeping the nation, and by the early 1980s, The Speakeasy had developed a reputation as Lexington's top "singles bar". Every weekend the club was filled to capacity with men and women, primarily in their thirties, forties, and fifties who were looking to mingle, dance, drink, and quite often, lose their inhibitions.

As Sean and his classmates entered the club, he noticed that the music was loud, the lights were bright and colorful, and many of the patrons, most of whom were women, were beautiful. He had never been in a dance club before, and he absorbed all of the sights and sounds, most of which were new to him. Beams of bright, colored light flashed across the room, reflecting occasionally off of the giant disco ball that dangled over the dance floor. The DJ was perched in a booth that seemed to levitate over the corner of the dance floor. Women were dancing, drinking, laughing and looked to be having the time of their lives. There was a tremendous energy in the room, and Sean was enthralled by it all.

As Kara led the other girls to the dance floor, Sean found a table not far the bar. He was soon joined by Ben, who could now barely keep his eyes open due to the vast quantity of beer he had consumed throughout the evening. As Ben wavered on the brink of passing out, Sean felt a tap on his shoulder. He turned in his seat to see Rob standing there.

"I know you," Rob said, shouting over the music. "Didn't we go to high school together?"

"We did," Sean shouted back. "You're Rob Caldwell, right? I'm Sean

Everett. I was a few years behind you in school."

"I remember you," Rob said somewhat coldly.

A bouncer began to remove Ben, who just then had passed out in his chair, when the girls arrived from the dance floor to help carry him out.

"Are you coming?" Kara asked Sean as they began to leave.

"I think I'm going to stay a little longer if that's all right," Sean answered.

"Sure," replied Kara with a smile. "We're going to get Ben back to his dorm - he's had a bit too much to drink, in case you haven't noticed."

"Do you need any help?" Sean asked.

"We're good, but thanks," Kara replied, as she handed Sean a cocktail napkin. "I'm staying in town this summer. Call me if you want to get together sometime."

Sean nodded, looked at the napkin, and placed it in the front pocket of his blue jeans. He then sat back down at the table, as did Rob, who was drinking a gin and tonic. Rob hadn't changed much since high school, with his dark hair and dark complexion. In the bar light, Rob had a passing resemblance to a young Elvis Presley, but rather than a sequined jumpsuit and cape, Rob was wearing a shimmering, gray button down shirt, black slacks, and a beeper attached to his belt.

The pair talked for a few minutes, catching up a little before the DJ announced last call. At that point, an exodus of patrons began spilling past the tables and into the street. Rob suggested that the two get coffee, and Sean agreed. At a nearby diner, Sean listened as Rob detailed his life since high school, about how he had spent his last few years working as a car salesman at a large automobile dealership on the east end of town. Before long, the conversation transitioned to the topic of women, which piqued Sean's interest a great deal. He was curious to hear what type of experiences Rob had encountered over the last few years. He wanted to know if the blowhard lothario from high school had managed to transform into the accomplished Don Juan he no doubt longed to be.

Under the stark fluorescent lights that cascaded from the ceiling, Rob was all too happy to share his recent experiences with Sean. With the same smugness from high school, Rob told Sean that he had bedded numerous women since high school, most of whom he had met by trolling The Speakeasy. He regaled Sean with stories of his conquests, including details of many of his encounters with various types of women. Rob's stories ranged from simple pick-ups at the club to much more exotic encounters, many of which included group sex, sex in public, and sex in unusual places. Beyond being a braggart, it was clear that Rob was truly obsessed with his pursuit of the opposite sex. Sean eagerly listened to Rob detail his exploits, fascinated by not only the stories but also the storyteller. He was entertained, but he still wondered how much of these tales were fact or fiction.

"Listening is the key," Rob said, reiterating the same mantra that Sean overheard in the high school cafeteria years earlier. "Women don't want to hear you talk, especially about yourself. They want you to listen to them while they talk - that's the key. That's the secret."

"And why is that?" asked Sean, playing the part of the willing protégé'.

"Women love to talk," Rob continued. "They love to talk about their feelings, their emotions, their hopes, their dreams. But most of all, they like to talk about their problems.

"So they want you to fix their problems?" Sean asked innocently.

"No, just the opposite," countered Rob. "Don't get involved - just listen and agree. If you fix one problem, three different ones will take its place. That's the way most women are wired. They want a sounding board, not solutions."

"What if they ask for help with a problem?" Sean asked, as he took a sip of his coffee.

"Then that's a little different," answered Rob. "If a woman asks you for help with a particular issue, make her be specific about the type of help she wants you to provide for her. Do only what is asked of you, even if you think you know a better way that can remedy the situation. Keep your mouth shut and do what you're asked to do - or told to do."

Sean nodded and continued to listen to Rob, who was still talkative despite the late hour. The conversation diverted to cars, sports, and other subjects, all of which Rob claimed expertise in, which amused Sean more than it impressed him. Still, Sean was enjoying his time with this smooth-talking, confident man who seemed to know everything about everything, especially women. By 4 a.m., the diner emptied out as the two men began to conclude their conversation. The server stopped by their booth, dropped off their check, and Rob pulled his wallet out of his pants.

"You free tomorrow night?" Rob asked, as he slipped some cash under the check. "Why don't you meet me at the club? I'll teach you a few things. Show you the ropes."

"Okay," Sean replied.

The next evening, The Speakeasy was alive again with the same energy that Sean had remembered from the night before. The music was infectious, with its primal beats and catchy melodies. The colorful lights flashed frantically across the dance floor, which was filled with a slew of sweaty bodies that were moving in perfect rhythm with the sounds that were pumping out of the speaker cabinets that were dangling from the ceiling above. The club was packed, and the hundreds of patrons gathered within were practically on top of each other. Some were seated at the tables that surrounded the dance floor, but others, including Sean and Rob, were standing at the bar. The men ordered their drinks and began scoping out the various women that were inside the club. Sean stood rigidly, looking somewhat uncomfortable, while Rob was relaxed. As he peered out at the dance floor, Rob commanded the room - exuding confidence as he held his gin and tonic.

"Black dress, 3 o'clock," Rob shouted. Sean looked out and saw two pretty brunettes, one in a black dress and the other in a blue blouse, gyrating playfully in the middle of the dance floor. Both were laughing, flipping their hair flirtatiously, and trying not to spill the drinks they were holding as they swayed along to the music.

Rob left the bar, bobbing his head with the music as he walked towards the women. Once they saw him, he raised his hands and began to dance with them, smiling and mimicking their moves as the song continued to play. When the music ended, he walked them back to their table, and then motioned Sean over to join them.

Sean was nervous at first, but began to feel at ease after Rob introduced him to the ladies, who were both vivacious and beautiful. Rob drove the conversation, especially with Sherri, the woman in the black dress who Rob spotted from across the room. Her friend Melinda took an instant liking to Sean, and with little provocation, convinced him to buy them a round of drinks. Sherri and Melinda were friends as well as co-workers - both taught at the same local elementary school - and they were out tonight celebrating Sherri's recent divorce. The four spent several hours at the club, drinking, dancing, and laughing, and when closing time arrived, Rob invited them to come back to his house to join him and Sean for a drink. They accepted his invitation, which came as a pleasant surprise to Sean.

Rob's house was a 2-story home located in a subdivision just east of downtown, which made it a short, convenient drive from the club. It was a typical bachelor pad, with lots of black leather furniture, as well as an eclectic array of cheap artwork that looked like it had been purchased at a department store. The women found great joy in teasing him about the samurai sword display that was mounted on his wall, but they enjoyed themselves nonetheless. After a couple more drinks, Sherri strongly hinted that it was very late, and that she and Melinda were in no shape to drive home. Rob asked if they would like to stay the night, and they obliged. Not long after, Rob took Sherri upstairs to his room while Sean and Melinda made themselves comfortable in the guest room. Melinda felt at ease with Sean, finding him to be trusting and good-hearted. They laughed at the many things they had in common, such as their mutual love of golf and Mexican food. They both laughed hysterically at the riotous noises of Rob and Sherri having sex upstairs. After a series of loud screams and moans, the sounds subsided, and then it was Sean and Melinda's turn. As they began to make love, Sean couldn't resist mocking Rob and Sherri by imitating their grunts and groans. Melinda soon joined in, and they had a good laugh at their friends' expense. Before long, however, the laughs subsided and they were focused entirely on each other. They made love, and then fell asleep shortly thereafter.

Melinda was only the third woman that Sean had ever had sex with, and his previous two experiences were largely forgettable. In high school, he lost his virginity to Marissa Fields, a tall, slender girl with long, curly brown hair and a toothy smile. It happened in the modest hotel room on prom of his senior year. They dated briefly afterward, but ended their relationship mutually just before graduation. He kept in touch with Marissa briefly, but last he heard she was studying to be a veterinarian at Auburn University. The second time was with "Courtney" - Sean never found out what her last name was. She was a red-haired "hippie chick" that hung out in the lobby of his dormitory during his freshman year of college. With her mellow speech and overly relaxed disposition, Courtney always seemed to be high on something. She was sweet and good-natured though, and loved watching local bands play. One night she invited Sean to a nearby college pub to hear a local group perform and he accepted. Later that evening she spent the night with him, but she disappeared the next morning. He saw her a few times after that, usually on campus, but she acted awkwardly around him. Although he didn't have feelings for her, Sean wondered if he had done something wrong that night - either conversationally or sexually - to make her not want to see him anymore.

The sun crept quietly through the blinds of Rob's living room window, and Sean awoke to the smell of coffee. The men said goodbye to Sherri and Melinda, both of whom were sluggish and hung over, and Sean left the house a few minutes later. He returned to his dormitory, showered, and took a nap. Later that evening, Rob called.

"You free next weekend?" he asked Sean, with a devilish tone in his voice.

"Definitely," Sean replied in a similar tone.

The following weekend, and every weekend that summer, Rob and Sean returned to The Speakeasy. Each evening played out like the last, as the pair would meet various women, wooing them within the walls of the club, then bringing them back to Rob's house to take them to bed. After their women departed, the men would usually go out for coffee or lunch, where Rob would recount the details of the previous night. Rob took great enjoyment in reliving each conquest through his conversations with Sean, but he took greater enjoyment in peppering the talks with lessons, as if Rob was a professor and Sean was his pupil. He shared his strategies and observations with Sean, bragging about his ability to not just read women, but to understand everything about them.

By mid-summer, the duo had developed a notorious reputation among the club's regular female clientele as pickup artists. Women found them to be an irresistible pair, seeing Sean as the "nice guy" who you would want to take home to meet your mother, and Rob as the "bad boy" who you would want to keep away from your mother - partly because she might want to steal him away from you and keep him for her own.

Despite their popularity, some of the ladies were not so thrilled to see them when they made return trips to the club. These women began putting the word out about Rob and Sean to other female guests at the club, which made it difficult for the men to continue their pursuit of one-night stands. The pair decided that they needed a brief break from the Speakeasy, "to let the heat die down," as Rob put it, so they decided to take their talents elsewhere. Rob had heard about a place called the Post, which was a lounge located inside a hotel on Lexington's north side, so he and Sean paid a visit there one evening to see what it had to offer. Much like the Speakeasy, there was music, a DJ, a dance floor, and a vast array of women, most of whom had never met either Rob or Sean. After a few successful weekends at the Post, the men began returning occasionally to the Speakeasy.

By summer's end, as both his confidence and conquests had grown, Sean was every bit the Casanova that Rob was. Sean had studied his every move and was developing a few of his own, much to the delight of his mischievous mentor.

"Now the student has become the teacher," cackled Rob one night at The Speakeasy, as he watched Sean confidently approach a pair of women who were seated near the dance floor. Rob typically was the "icebreaker" in their partnership, approaching the women first and then inviting Sean over to join them once the conversation was established.

The men became good friends as a result of their weekend escapades, providing something to each other that had been missing in their lives. Even though he was constantly surrounded with female company, Rob was lonely. To him, Sean wasn't just a "running buddy", as Rob used to often call him, but he was also his best friend. For Sean, he felt alive for the first time in his life. This world of seduction had seduced him as well, and he was enjoying every minute of it.

For two years they continued as barflies at the club, and their social successes continued. Week in and week out, Rob grew more immersed in this world. Sean, however, was becoming slowly disenchanted by it. These experiences had given him so much, but moreover they had helped him grow as a person. He wanted something more - something real - and he knew that he wouldn't be able to find it within the walls of a night club. His life had become a party, but parties have to come to an end sometime. He had always been wary of the fact that the environment Rob had created for himself was an empty existence, and that someday soon he wouldn't feel comfortable in that world. Rather than thinking about the endless stream of passionate nights with beautiful strangers, Sean began to dwell on the negatives of the life that he had chosen - from the small things, like the extremely late nights and extremely painful hangovers, to the larger things, like the fear of getting a DUI or catching an STD. Through it all, Sean always wrestled with his conscience about the life he was leading, but now he was considering letting his conscience win.

As he finished his senior year of college, Sean got a job and entered the work force. He was still trolling The Speakeasy with Rob, but his heart was no longer in it. When the club hosted its annual Halloween party that year, Sean and Rob were there as usual. Virtually everyone inside the club was dressed in costumes, including Sean, garbed in a police costume complete with mirrored sunglasses, and Rob, in a white Elvis jumpsuit that made him look even more like the king of rock n' roll than he already did. As Rob disappeared onto the dance floor to romance a Marilyn Monroe lookalike, Sean stood up from his seat at the bar, and accidentally bumped into a tall blonde woman clad in a skintight, black cat suit, spilling her drink in the process.

"I'm sorry," Sean said, "let me buy you a drink - what are you having?"

"It's okay, I'm fine," the woman responded, as she wiped her sleeve with a napkin.

"Please, I insist," Sean continued playfully. "You wouldn't want to get in trouble for resisting an officer, would you?"

"Ha ha, very funny," she said. "Okay, you win. It's a cranberry and vodka."

Sean flagged down the bartender and bought the beautiful cat woman a drink, as well as one for himself. He glanced over at Rob, who was now sitting at a table near the dance floor with "Marilyn", engaging in conversation with her and her two girlfriends, who appeared to both be dressed as pirate wenches. Knowing that Rob would likely be occupied for a while, he offered the cat woman the open seat that was next to him, and the pair sat down.

"I'm Sean," he said, extending his hand to introduce himself.

"Pleased to meet you, Sean," she said, as she gracefully extended her hand. "I'm Jaclyn."

As the night progressed and he talked with the young woman, he found himself hanging on her every word, and laughing at her every joke. To Sean, It seemed like they were the only two people in the room - he couldn't hear the music or see the flashing disco lights because he was so focused on her. She made him nervous, but in a good way - and this was exciting to him. There was definitely something special about her, something different, and he was beyond intrigued by her. He could actually feel himself falling in love with this winsome woman clad in a cat suit.

After finishing their drinks, Sean asked her if she would like to go across the street to the smaller, quieter Irish pub, so they could continue their conversation. She obliged, and as they left the club, Sean looked at Rob and waved goodbye. To his surprise, Rob was glaring back at him, almost in disapproval. He nodded to Sean, and lowered his head. Rob felt lonely as he sank into his seat, surrounded by the music and mayhem, and "Marilyn", who ran her white feather boa across his neck in an effort to cheer him up.

That was the last evening that Sean ever went to The Speakeasy, and it was also the last time he had ever seen Rob - until tonight.

Four

"So you married that girl - the one from the bar that night, right?" asked Rob, as he finished his first glass of bourbon and started pouring his second.

"I did," Sean replied. "We married a couple years later and were together fifteen years. We have a boy - his name is Braden."

"Braden," Rob said, as he squinted his eyes. "I like that name."

"But," continued Sean as he refilled his glass as well, "as of this week, the marriage is officially over. And today I lost my job, so right now you're looking at a man right now who has definitely seen better days."

"Ouch," Rob replied, as he folded his arms.

"I'd been working as a broker for Kenley and Logan for the last few years, but business has been tailing off a bit," Sean said. "They told me this morning. I didn't even see it coming."

"Oh well," said Rob, "all's well that end's well."

Rob smiled, leaned forward and raised his glass for an impromptu toast. Sean stared at Rob, hesitant at first, then he shrugged, smiled, and clinked his glass against Rob's. The two then each took a large gulp from their glasses.

"How much do you have saved up?" Rob asked.

"Enough to get me through the next month or two," replied Sean, "but after that, I don't know what I'm going to do. I got to keep the house, but the payments on it are huge. She got half of our savings, and the child support payment was figured up when I was working. All in all, it's not pretty."

"Can you draw unemployment?" asked Rob.

"I wish I could," said Sean, "but a few years ago my company restructured, and they asked me if I would be interested in working for them as a subcontractor rather than as a salaried employee. I was making a really good living at the time, but as contract labor I knew that the potential was there to make a lot more money - free me up to do a little freelance work if I wanted. I accepted their offer, and the money was great for a while. But now, because I technically wasn't an employee..."

"Because you weren't an employee, you're not eligible for unemployment," Rob interrupted, finishing his friend's sentence.

"Exactly," Sean said.

"The devil's in the details," added Rob.

"Really? I thought he was sitting in my kitchen," Sean coyly remarked as Rob smiled and shook his head. Sean walked around and sat down at the counter next to his friend.

"Anyhow," Sean continued, "I'll start sending my resume' out on Monday. Surely somebody out there is willing to hire me."

"Maybe sooner than later," answered Rob, as he leaned back in his barstool.

"If you don't mind me asking, why are you here?" Sean asked, as he took another drink from his glass. "I haven't seen you in ages and then all of a sudden you're in my house?"

"What if I told you that I had the answer to all of your problems?" Rob asked in a very serious tone. "What if I told you that I had a job for you that will fix this financial mess that you're in - right now - and you would get to have a lot of fun in the process?"

"I'm listening," Sean replied, intrigued but skeptical at the same time.

"I was selling cars for years after our time at The Speakeasy had come to an end," Rob continued. "I was good at it, really good - but after a while it was boring. I even started hating it. But then one day a lady walked into the dealership - she was a little older than me, and very attractive. She wanted me to show her almost our whole inventory, from the most expensive, loaded SUVs to the cheapest economy cars we had on the lot. We spent all afternoon test-driving every make and model that we had in that joint. What I didn't realize at the time was that she was testing me. She kept goading me into trying to sell her one of these cars, saying things like 'make me want to buy it' and 'sell it to me.' I started out by giving her the canned sales speech I'd done a thousand times before, but it wasn't working on her. I couldn't figure her out, and it was pissing me off."

"That's a switch," Sean remarked. "Normally you're the one pissing women off, not the other way around."

"True," said Rob, nodding in agreement. "By the end of the day, I decided to throw my sales training out the window and try a different technique with her. I told her that I could tell by the way she carried herself that she was a woman who was used to getting what she wanted. So I asked her if there was anything I could do to make her buy a car from me that day. She shot a wicked smile at me and told me that she would buy something from me if I got down on my hands and knees in the middle of the showroom and begged her to buy a car. I was stunned at first - I didn't want to humiliate myself like that in front of my co-workers. So I got ready to tell her off when I noticed something in her eyes that I can't explain. Up to that point, she had shown me a lot of different sides of her - charming and flirtatious one minute, cold and aggressive the next. I wanted to tell her off, but then when I looked into her eyes, I realized that I just couldn't. She had a power over me unlike anything that I've ever experienced. It was like some kind of mind control, or voodoo shit - it was crazy. At that point, it went from beyond selling her a car to just wanting to make her happy. I realized that she had broken me, and there was nothing that I could do to resist her. So I dropped to the showroom floor and began groveling on my hands and knees, right there in front of her and in front of the other salesmen and customers. They were all laughing at me, but I didn't care.

I just wanted to please her - that's all that mattered to me."

"Wow, did she buy a car?" Sean asked.

"Even better," Rob replied. "She gave me my freedom. She ended up getting a Lexus, a really nice one mind you, and while filling out the paperwork at my desk, she told me that she wanted me to leave the dealership and come work for her. So I did, and I've been working for her ever since."

"Doing what?" inquired Sean.

"I'm a Blue Shirt," Rob replied.

"What's a 'Blue Shirt'?" Sean asked, obviously intrigued.

"Blue Shirts is the name of her company," Rob continued. "It's a 'transportation' business, more or less."

"'More or less'?" echoed Sean with his question. "What do you mean exactly?"

"There are a number of women in the thoroughbred business that live out of state, or out of the country," Rob replied. "When they come to Kentucky, whether it's for business or just to visit, they contact us and we provide them with a professional driver to take them around town."

"Women only?" Sean inquired, as he meandered over to his refrigerator and plucked some ice cubes from the freezer. "That seems a bit unusual."

"It's an unusual business," Rob replied glibly.

"Why is it called Blue Shirts?" asked Sean.

"Our drivers have a strict dress code," answered Rob. "When they are working, they must wear a blue dress shirt, as well as a tie, dress pants, dress shoes. It's kind of our uniform."

"I see," Sean said, as he dropped the ice cubes into his empty glass. "So would be a chauffer? No offense, but I didn't think that they made that much money."

"Actually, there's a bit more to the job than just that," Rob continued. "We cater exclusively to women who are traveling alone and desire companionship for the few days that they are in town. Our drivers are expected to not only transport our clients around the city, but to also entertain them as well. Typically this means spending all day and all night with them, doing whatever they ask of you."

"Like what?" asked Sean.

"It can be anything really," replied Rob. "Most of the time you're taking them to dinner, attending parties with them as their date, or driving them around the countryside to see the sights. Last week I had a client take me shopping with her. You're mainly there to provide good company and conversation."

"I don't know," Sean replied, "I've never driven a limousine before."

"Actually, our drivers use their own vehicles," Rob remarked. "We only drive black, newer model SUVs, like Escalades or Suburbans. Like the one that you have parked in the driveway."

Sean smiled again. "You said 'all day and all night'?" he asked. "What typically happens at night?"

"You take them back to their hotel room and sleep with them," Rob said.

"I beg your pardon?" Sean asked, as he nearly spit up the drink of bourbon he was taking. "You're kidding, right?"

"Many of our clients are single, divorced, widowed - some are married, happily or otherwise," continued Rob, "but without exception, they are all expecting to have sex with the driver that's assigned to them when they are in town."

"So you came here tonight to ask me to be a prostitute?" Sean inquired, as his eyebrows furrowed and he set his glass of bourbon on the kitchen counter.

"Sean, it's your ticket out of the mess that you're in," Rob replied, pleading his case. "These women are very wealthy, and they pay a lot of money for our services - a lot of money. Look, I know that this is a lot to digest right now..."

"A lot to digest?" interrupted Sean, with a sarcastic tone in his voice. "What even made you think that I would be interested in doing something like this?"

"Because you're good at it," answered Rob. "You know how to make a woman feel like she's the most important person in the world. You have everything that it takes to be successful with the company - looks, charm, experience - you're the whole package."

"That was a long time ago," Sean countered.

"Look, I'll be honest," Rob said, rising from his seat, "I still keep in touch with some of the guys from school, and one of them told me about you getting divorced. Then last week I was downtown at a stoplight and saw you in the lane next to me. I hadn't seen you in years, but I recognized you. You were sitting there in your car, staring off into the distance - with a blank expression on your face. For someone driving such a nice car and wearing such a nice suit, you looked unhappy. You looked like how I remembered you when we first started hanging out together. It was at that point I knew that I needed to bring the old Sean back - the fun, confident guy that you became after we became friends. That's the guy who I remember, not the shell of a man that's getting drunk in his kitchen on a Friday night. You're better than this."

"This is crazy, not to mention illegal," Sean replied. "Aren't you worried about getting arrested - or going to jail?"

"We're the best-kept secret around," Rob said. "Our clients go through a very strict screening process, and we only hire people that we know we can trust. It also helps that we're a small, tight-knit operation. We've been flying under the radar for years, and that's the way we like it. But business has picked up quite a bit recently, so much so that we need to hire another driver - immediately."

"Look Rob, I appreciate the offer, but it's just not for me," Sean replied. "It sounds like what you're proposing could help me, it really could - but at the end of the day I'm a father, and I'm not willing to risk my relationship with my son just to make a fast buck. I'll find work soon, and eventually I'll dig myself out of this hole. I'm sorry, I just can't."

"I understand," Rob replied, "but my offer still stands."

Rob reached for Sean's cell phone, which was resting near the edge of the counter, and began to press its buttons. "Here's my phone number," Rob said, "call me when you change your mind."

"Don't you mean if I change my mind?" asked a smiling Sean.

Rob didn't answer the question - instead he just smiled and walked to the front door to let himself out.

Five

It was Sunday morning, and Sean was in Midway, a quaint little town just west of Lexington. He was sitting in a booth at his father's favorite restaurant, rubbing his eyes and glancing at the menu. He was a little hung over, but he had agreed a few days earlier to meet his father for a late breakfast that morning, and he didn't want to cancel plans with him at the last minute. As he looked around the room, with its dark hardwood floors and its garnet-colored walls, he caught a whiff of bacon drifting through the air. It made him hungry. Just then, the door of the restaurant opened, revealing an older man that Sean knew well.

"How are you, Sean?" asked the familiar voice. It was Sean's father, Jack Everett, who took off his coat, and slowly slid into the booth.

"I'm well, how are you?" Sean replied.

"Hungry," Jack said, letting out a laugh.

Jack was a thin man in his mid-sixties, with short gray hair and a warm smile. He was somewhat of a local legend - a longtime police officer for the city of Lexington who was forced to resign during a much-publicized internal affairs investigation in the 1980s. The department was embroiled in corruption, riddled with officers who were routinely planting, tampering with and stealing evidence. Jack was an honest cop, but his partner and close friend, Billy Spradlin, was not. Charges were brought against Spradlin for evidence tampering and the district attorney's case was strong, but they needed Jack to take the stand and testify against his partner to ensure a conviction.

Jack was very vocal about not wanting to testify against Spradlin. Although e knew that his partner was guilty of the charges that were brought against him, he elieved that it was wrong to turn against his friend. "Billy had my back a million nes," he would later tell his friends, "so I've got his back on this one."

When called to the stand, Jack refused to answer any of the district attorney's uestions. The judge ruled that he was in contempt of court, which landed him in il for almost a week before the ruling was overturned. Without Jack's testimony, e jury found Billy Spradlin not guilty, sparking public outrage. Spradlin retired om the department soon after, but Jack was suspended and later fired. He filed it against the City of Lexington for being "unjustly terminated", and received large sum of money when it was settled out of court. Ironically, Billy Spradlin sappeared into anonymity and hadn't been heard from in nearly 30 years.

Sean was a young boy at the time of the trial, and was shielded from most its details by his mother, Kathleen, who stood by Jack during the entire ordeal.

"How's Mom?" asked Sean, as he settled into his seat.

"She's doing well, says to tell you 'hi'," Jack replied. "She's out shopping day for Braden - you know how much she loves that grandson of hers. I was oping you'd have him with you this morning."

"He's with Jaclyn this weekend," Sean replied. "It's probably a good thing o. I lost my job on Friday and haven't been in the best mood."

"What happened?" asked Jack.

Sean proceeded to tell his father about his dismissal, as well as his plans start looking for a new job the next day. As the server took their orders, Sean emed cautiously optimistic about his chances to find work. "It's just a matter of me," he said. "The market is slow right now, but with my experience I should find mething."

After taking a sip of his coffee, Jack coughed deeply - a low, rumbling cough at echoed throughout the nearly empty restaurant.

"Are you okay?" Sean asked. "You're actually looking a little pale th
morning too - maybe you should see a doctor."

"I already have, son," replied Jack. "That's why I wanted to see you th
morning."

"What is it?" asked Sean in a comforting tone.

"I hadn't been feeling too well the last few days," Jack muttered. "You
mother thought it might be pneumonia - you know how she likes to worry. I wer
to the doctor, he took a couple of x-rays, and found a spot on my lung. It's cancer

Sean was devastated. His entire relationship with his father flashed befor
his eyes. He started to choke up, leaning in towards his dad and placing his elbow
on the table.

"What else did they tell you?" he asked.

"Well, the good news is that it looks like they've caught it kind of early, s
at least it's treatable," Jack said. "But the bad news is that your mother isn't going t
let me smoke cigars around the house anymore."

"Is there anything that you need?" Sean asked. "Anything at all I can do?"

"I've got health insurance through the VA," Jack replied. "It should cove
just about anything I need, plus your mother and I have a good amount saved u
if things run over a bit."

"How is she handling it?" Sean asked, as Jack cleared his throat again.

"Oh, about as well as can be expected," Jack replied. "She used to be
nurse, so she thinks that she knows everything of course. I have another appointmer
coming up next week and she's going to come with me - probably going to tell th
doctors how to do their job."

Both men smiled again, as Jack began to nibble on a piece of toast. Sea
sunk his fork into his western omelet and then glanced up at his father, who clearl

lidn't have much of an appetite. It was a strange feeling to know that his father was
ick, and to see that his body was weakened. Sean's mind was filled with thoughts
of his childhood and all of the wonderful memories he had with his dad. As he took
another bite of his breakfast, Sean remembered him as the strong, young man who
taught him to ride a bicycle, hit a baseball, and drive a car.

Fearing becoming emotional in front of his father, he wanted to change the
subject, or at least the direction of the conversation. His thoughts drifted briefly to
the talk that he had the night before with Rob.

"Dad," Sean asked, "You're a really good man. I've always looked up to
you and I always will, but I need to ask you something. When you were a cop, and
they asked you to testify against your friend - you knew that he was a dirty cop. You
saw him do things that were against the law, yet you went to jail to protect him.
Why?"

Jack reasoned with his fork then looked at Sean. "It's true, Billy Spradlin
broke the law," Jack said, "but the men that he put behind bars were much more
dangerous than he ever was. At that time, the streets were filled with some of the
worst criminals you had ever laid eyes on - murderers, drug dealers, thieves that
would rob you and then shoot you for the hell of it. We would arrest them, but
they'd be back out on the street the next day. It was the court system that needed to
be on trial, not Billy. He did what he needed to do so he could keep those bastards
off the street and out of our homes and schools. He made the city a safer place."

Sean nodded slowly as his father continued. "The law isn't perfect, son,"
Jack said. "It's just a set of ideas that are open to interpretation. It can guide you,
but that doesn't mean that you have to follow it blindly. Sometimes the right choice
is to not play by the rules."

Sean nodded again, and both men finished their breakfasts. As they began
to leave, Sean grabbed the bill that the server had placed on the table before his
father could reach it. Both men smiled, and as Sean opened his wallet, he looked
inside and saw that he didn't have any cash. He looked up at his father, and then
back down at his wallet. He began to pull a credit card from his wallet when Jack
placed a $20 bill on the table next to the check.

"It's okay, Dad, I've got this," Sean protested.

"You can get it next time," Jack replied, as he took a final sip of coffee. "This one's on me."

His father rose slowly from the booth, put on his coat, and steadied himself against the back of the booth. The men waved to the restaurant staff and walked out to the sidewalk. As Sean walked his father to his car, the two men were surprised to see a few flakes of snow falling from the sky.

"Wow, that sure is pretty," Jack said, as he marveled at the snow as it fell gracefully towards the earth. Both men smiled and hugged, and then Jack entered his car.

"I'll see you soon," Sean said, as he closed the car door for his father.

Later that evening, Sean found himself in his living room, seated on his couch and surrounded by a stack of papers and his laptop computer. To his left was a copy of his resume', as well as a handwritten list of local brokerage firms that he planned to contact in the morning. To his right was his checkbook, sitting squarely on a stack of bills. With his calculator in his lap, he opened the envelopes, removed the invoices within, and started adding up their amounts. He had just enough in his checkbook to cover paying the electric, water, internet and satellite TV, but he realized that he didn't have enough money to pay the remaining bills in the stack. After scrutinizing his credit card statement, he raised his head and looked at the ceiling in frustration and desperation. He hadn't even made it to the bottom of the stack yet, where the mortgage and truck payments were lurking.

He got up from the couch and walked slowly through his house. Jaclyn had taken most of the furniture, which gave the house an emptiness that made it feel foreign to him. The walls were also missing practically all of the pictures, which further added to the emptiness of the home. Sean found himself feeling empty as well - a combination of guilt and sadness began to overcome him as he began to think about the wonderful memories the family had shared in the house. He walked into Braden's room, and thoughts of his son raced through his mind. As Sean looked at the rocking chair in the corner of the room, he remembered reading books to Braden in that chair just before bedtime. He also recalled a poignant moment while he was tucking Braden into bed when he asked Sean "Daddy, if anything happens to you and Mommy, who will take care of me?"

"I will always take care of you," Sean told Braden that night. "As long as I'm on this earth, I will always make sure you are safe. You never have to worry about that."

Sean turned away and left Braden's room, walked back to the living room, and sat again on the couch. He lowered his head and put his hands over his eyes, but after a moment, he caught a glimpse of his cell phone resting on the end table. He looked at it, almost angrily, for what seemed like an hour before picking it up. "What am I getting myself into?" he said aloud to himself, took a deep breath, and called Rob.

Six

It was now Monday night, and the warmth of the past weekend was no more. The air was freezing cold, and a slight rain splattered across the windshield of Rob's truck. As he looked out of the window from the passenger seat, Sean watched as the farms and trees of the countryside gave way to the suburbs, and then eventually to the buildings that inhabited downtown. There was hardly any traffic, especially as they approached the homes in one the Lexington's oldest and most respected neighborhoods.

"We're almost there," Rob said as he piloted his vehicle through the messy streets. "She's excited about meeting you."

"I still can't believe I'm doing this," Sean remarked as he started buttoning his coat.

"You're going to be fine," Rob replied. "Trust me."

Rob parked on the street and the two men exited the vehicle. Sean looked around and could see that his friend had taken him to a part of town that was just a few blocks northwest of where he used to work as a stockbroker. This area was considered an historic district, with its old, large houses and their turn-of-the-century architecture. Scurrying along the sidewalk, they approached a large, 2-story white brick residence. Through the darkness and the rain, the pair approached the Victorian-styled home, which was shrouded somewhat by a pair of tall oak trees. The men walked up the narrow driveway, and Rob opened a small, black iron gate that led to the brick-covered path. They walked quickly to the front porch as the rain continued to splatter off of their coats.

"She's going to like you," Rob said assuredly, as he rang the doorbell.

"She's not going to make me get on my knees and sell her a car is she?" Sean asked with a smile. Moments later, the door opened, and a large man invited Rob and Sean inside.

"Good evening," said the figure, who was an African-American man, perhaps in his early thirties and sporting a shaved head and the physique of a bodybuilder. "Anjelica is expecting you. Follow me."

Rob and Sean entered the home and followed the large man, who was clad in a white sleeveless t-shirt and black slacks. They passed through the foyer, which had a beautiful staircase and large chandelier hanging high above them from the ceiling. As they walked through a small hallway towards the back of the house, Sean noticed that the home had a vintage feel to it, with its hardwood floors and antique tables. He passed by a few oil paintings that were framed ornately in the hallway of the foyer, most of which looked old and expensive. Suddenly, the men made their way into a large, dimly lit room in the back of the house.

As Sean entered the room, he looked to the left and saw two large, antique tables at opposite ends of the room, as well as a pair of large, dark cherry bookcases. Next to one of the cabinets was an old Victrola record player, positioned closely to a tall, skinny brass lamp. The walls were made of dark wood, and silk turquoise curtains hung from the windows. A large, plush white rug covered some of the floor, and a solitary doorway led into an unseen corridor near the corner of the room. A very large oil painting was displayed prominently in a gold frame, hanging just above a hand-carved shelf. The painting, which looked to be an antique as well, was clearly the centerpiece of the room. Upon its canvas was the image of a well-dressed brunette woman, garbed elegantly in a black dress and black hat that had dark feathers protruding from its top. The woman, and the portrait itself, looked to be from the 1800s. Her face was almost expressionless, save for a slight smile that would draw comparisons to the Mona Lisa.

To his right, Sean saw another part of the room entirely. The darkened walnut walls gave way to a fireplace, and within it was a warm, crackling fire that illuminated the room with a slow, flickering array of light. A brass poker and dark wooded bellow were leaning against the gray, stacked stone that surrounded the fireplace. An oval mirror, lined with deer antlers, hung on the wall near th fireplace. There were two red, antique sofas in the middle of the room, arrange evenly across a large Oriental rug, and beyond that was a large bay window, whic was surrounded by a turquoise drapery. On one side of the window was a large English-style grandfather clock, made of dark cherry wood. On the other side of th window was a woman, standing motionless as she peered into the darkness of he back yard, watching the rain as it caromed off the glass and onto the back porch.

"Excuse me, Madam," the large man announced, "your guests are here."

"Thank you, Samson," the woman said, as she turned away from the windov and approached the men. Samson smiled at her and took the men's coats. He the delivered a smirk to both Rob and Sean before exiting the room.

"He likes me," Rob whispered to Sean sarcastically.

"Tonight's weather is just like a woman, is it not?" asked the mysteriou woman, while running a finger over the glass of wine she was holding in her hanc "Hot one minute and cold the next."

Anjelica, who appeared to be in her early fifties, was elegant and beautifu Her slim figure was accentuated snugly by her black dress, and the strand of whit pearls around her plunging neckline made her seem almost regal in appearance Her hair was long and dark, except for a small river of gray which wound itsel down her head and ended tucked behind her ear. With her deep brown eyes and strong jaw line, she looked like a member of the Kennedy family, and that sh would probably be more at home in a Massachusetts mansion rather than a histori Kentucky home.

She motioned for the men to take a seat, and then proceeded to pou them both a glass of wine. She took the first glass to Rob, who had made himsel comfortable on an antique, plush velvet chair. As she handed the glass to Rob, sh gave him a slow, lingering kiss on the mouth. Sean turned his head away, slightl embarrassed at what he was seeing, and took a seat on a dark red love seat just few feet away from his friend. The woman walked over to Sean, handed him a glas of wine, and sat next to him on the love seat.

"I'm Anjelica," she said. "You must be Sean. It's so good to meet you." She extended her hand gracefully and Sean shook it. "Rob speaks very highly of you," she continued, "and I've found him to be an impeccable judge of character." She then placed her hand on his knee and looked at him, with a playful glint in her eye.

"It's good to meet you too," Sean said nervously. "And I appreciate the opportunity that you're giving me. I hope that I won't disappoint you."

"I'm sure you won't," she said, taking another sip of her wine.

"Sean here is ready, willing, and able," Rob said, as he casually threw one of his legs across the ottoman.

"He seems ready and willing," she replied, glaring at Rob. She then turned her face again towards Sean, staring into his eyes. "But is he able?"

"Just tell me what I need to know," he answered, trying his best to look comfortable and confident to his hostess.

"How much did Rob tell you about our little enterprise?" asked Anjelica.

"Just the basics, I suppose" Sean replied. "I have a few questions though, if you don't mind me asking."

"Certainly," replied Anjelica, "but first I need your phone."

Looking puzzled, Sean removed his cell phone from his pocket and handed it to her. He watched as her fingers maneuvered their way across its screen, and his focus shifted to Rob, who was still sporting a devilish smile.

"The love seat," said Anjelica, still swiping her fingers across Sean's phone. "Do you like it? It belonged to Belle Brezing, the famous Lexington madam. Many of the items in this house were hers as well, including the portrait that I caught you admiring when you entered the room."

"It's nice," Sean replied, as she handed him back his phone.

"Belle was a woman before her time," said Anjelica, turning her head and looking at the large portrait across the room. "A true entrepreneur."

"Like yourself," added Rob, eliciting a smile from Anjelica.

Sean was aware of Belle Brezing, a legendary local figure who had operated a handful of houses of ill repute in Lexington in the late 1800s and early 1900s. Although she notoriously made her living as a Madam, her popularity had continued over the years. It was said that celebrated author Margaret Mitchell used Belle Brezing as a strong influence in creating the character of Belle Watling for her book, Gone With the Wind.

"I just installed an application on your phone," she continued. "The app will signal you when you have an assignment. Each notification that I send you will have all of the essential information that you'll need - the client's name, her phone number, where and when to pick her up, where she'll be staying, and the length of her stay."

"How long do they usually stay?" asked Sean.

"In most cases it's three days, however sometimes it can be more," she replied. "It's expected that you accept all of the assignments I send you, however if you are deathly ill or have a similar unavoidable emergency, then you will need to let me know immediately so the client can be reassigned to another gentleman."

"I understand," replied Sean, nodding slowly.

"Typically our clients fly in Friday morning and fly out Monday morning, however that's not always set in stone," Anjelica added. "Are you available most weekends?"

"I can be," Sean said, as he glanced toward Rob and then looked back at Anjelica.

"I also put my contact information in your phone," she continued, "as you may call or text me with any questions that you may have. Do you have a Paypal account?"

"Yes," Sean replied.

"Excellent," she said. "After each completed assignment your payment will e transferred to you in this manner. Text me the email address for your account ater this evening if you don't mind."

"Certainly," Sean responded. "Rob mentioned that we use our own cars hen we're working? Is that right?"

"That's correct," replied Anjelica. "Technically we are a transportation usiness, so you will need a valid driver's license and a clean driving record. Have ou had any recent DUIs or major accidents?"

"No," replied Sean as he shook his head emphatically.

"Also, how long has it been since you've had an HIV test?" Anjelica inquired.

"I don't know," answered Sean, "I think I had to get one when I got married ut that was years ago."

"In that case I'll need you stop by the health department and have an HIV est performed," replied Anjelica. "It just takes a few minutes. I require that all of he gentlemen that work for me have the test done regularly."

"Okay, I'll take care of it" Sean said. "One last thing - everything lately has een such a blur that I forgot to ask how much I'll be getting paid."

Anjelica and Rob laughed. "An excellent question indeed," Anjelica replied. The price that our clients pay for a 3-day package is $10,000, of which you receive alf and I receive half.

"$5,000?" Sean asked, trying his best to contain his excitement.

"That's correct," she said. "After each assignment, I will send you your hare via Paypal. The clients also have the option to leave a tip at the conclusion of heir time with us, of which you receive 100%. These tips are usually a few hundred ollars - sometimes much more."

"So what do you say, Sean?" Rob interjected, still smiling as he slouched in his seat. "Do you think that this job is right for you?"

"I do," Sean replied, looking at his friend with a bit more confidence then he had when they first entered the house. Sean then turned back towards Anjelica. "When can I start?" he asked.

"Soon," she said. "Probably this week, or next week at the latest. The horses will be running again at Keeneland in April, which is almost three weeks away. As you might imagine, that's always one of our busiest times."

Sean was very familiar with Keeneland, the famous thoroughbred racing facility that was located near the airport on the west end of Lexington. He had taken clients there many times over the years, and he and Jaclyn had attended the races there on many occasions as well. He briefly imagined what it would be like to be seated trackside there now with a strange woman by his side.

"My schedule is wide open," Sean said to his new employer, who was smiling devilishly.

"That's what I like to hear," she said, as she finished her glass of wine and placed it on a nearby table. "One last thing," she said, as she pulled a white piece of paper from the drawer of the nearest end table. "This is an NDA, which I need you sign."

"An NDA?" queried Sean, glancing at Rob before looking back at Anjelica.

"A non-disclosure agreement," she answered. "It essentially says that you won't discuss any aspect of our company with anyone other than our clients or your fellow employees. If someone from the outside wants to know what you do, you can tell them you're a driver, a chauffer - whatever. You can never reveal anything about the actual services that we provide."

Rob nodded slowly, took the pen and paper, and signed his name at the bottom of the document. Anjelica walked the men back to her front door, making small talk as they made their way back through the narrow hallway. Samson was waiting by the door, handing the two men their coats and giving Sean a long, lingering stare. Rob opened the door, revealing the loud sounds of the rain striking the porch and the nearby sidewalk.

"Welcome to Blue Shirts," Anjelica said to Sean, who smiled and nodded at his new employer.

Sean then walked with Rob back into the darkness outside. While the men walked down the sidewalk to Rob's car, Sean's mind was racing. He was thinking about the money that he would be making while he worked for Anjelica, and how it would not only solve his financial problems, but it would solve them much faster than he initially thought possible. He thought of the bills that he had, which seemed insurmountable. He also thought of his father's declining health, and how he now might now be able to help him financially should those medical expenses get out of hand. Finally, he thought of Braden, and how he could continue to provide for him the way he did prior to the divorce.

"Well, that was interesting," Sean said sarcastically, buckling his seatbelt and placing his cold hands in his coat pockets. "I never in my life thought I would meet an actual madam, much less be working for one. What's her deal anyway?"

"She's a piece of work all right," Rob replied, as he turned the key of his ignition and began driving slowly down the dimly lit street. "Anjelica is from eastern Kentucky - Pikeville, I believe. She grew up on the wrong side of the tracks - her dad was a bootlegger, and was always in trouble with the law. He would get drunk and beat her brothers, hit her mom - he was a real son of a bitch. When she was old enough, she married a local boy just to get the hell out of that house. He found work in Lexington, so they moved here, but the marriage went south pretty soon after that."

"I know the feeling," Sean said, as he watched the windshield wipers brush away the miniature flakes of snow that continued to fall from the sky.

"She was what you would call a 'late bloomer'," Rob continued, as he adjusted the heater on his truck. "The shy, country girl from the holler, who as a teenager was awkward and pretty, suddenly became beautiful. At first she was scared of the attention, even somewhat confused by it because it seemed to happen almost overnight. But it didn't take her long to realize that she had a power over men that was overwhelming. This made her husband jealous of course. It drove him crazy, so much so that he couldn't handle it. He became possessive, and wouldn't let her go out, or have girlfriends. He was always afraid that she would cheat on him, but she never did. She loved him and was faithful to him, but he was always suspicious of her. She finally got fed up with him and divorced him a little while later."

"She's a very beautiful woman," added Sean, as he pulled his hands from his pockets and began rubbing them together.

"Not long after that, she found a sugar daddy," Rob continued. "He was very old and very rich. He made his millions in the coal industry, and in Anjelica he had finally found his trophy wife. When he died a couple years later, he left most of his fortune to her, making her a very wealthy widow at the tender age of twenty-eight. Even though she seemingly had everything that she could want, there was something missing. She had come a long way from her humble beginnings in eastern Kentucky, but she was filled with self-doubt. She wanted to be respected and admired, especially by the wealthy and powerful members of Lexington society. She hosted galas, made appearances at high-profile charity events, joined the country club, and tried her best to become part of these elite social circles, but she soon realized that they would never accept her. The women that comprised these circles looked down upon her, because of her poor upbringing and that she had married into money, despite the fact that many of these women had modest backgrounds before marrying into wealth. These women also saw Anjelica as a threat, because of her youth and her beauty. So they shunned her - treated her as an outcast who would never be 'good enough' to be a member of their group."

"She never got over that, did she?" asked Sean.

"No, she didn't" replied Rob. "But she still wanted to belong, and feel accepted. That's why she started Blue Shirts. Ironically, the very women who rejected her now line up in the street to buy what she's selling. Why? Because there's something missing in their lives and Anjelica is able to fulfill those needs. That's why they entrust her with their friendship, their money, and most importantly, their secrets."

Seven

It was Tuesday afternoon, and Sean was running errands before he had to pick Braden up from school. His first stop was Jaclyn's office.

Silver Lake Realty was nestled in a small wooded office park off on the south end of town, about ten miles from downtown. Sean walked into the lobby, walked past the receptionist, and made his way through the large room where most of the agents had desks. Most everyone there knew Sean, and either nodded to him or smiled as he walked by them. Most of them were on their phones, making lunch plans and scurrying about. Sean walked past the agents and into Jaclyn's office, which was towards the back of the building. It had a large window and a beautiful view of the trees and shrubs that were outside, all of which were evergreens that were just a few feet from the window pane. A young, enthusiastic couple was leaving Jaclyn's office as Sean entered, and by the sound of it she had just sold them their first home.

"Ahh, young love," Sean said, standing by her desk.

"I didn't expect to see you here today," Jaclyn said, still sitting in her chair.

"I was in the neighborhood and thought I'd bring you your check," he said, as he handed her an envelope.

"Thanks," she said, with a quizzical look on her face. "I actually wasn't expecting this today in light of your work situation and all."

"Well, it's looking like I've found a job," shared Sean. "I'll be starting in a few days, and if everything goes well, I should be able to stay on schedule with the child support payments. I'll mainly be working weekends, so if you can work with me on that I'd appreciate it. I don't think that it will be every weekend, but if that's the case, can we work out something where it doesn't affect my time with Braden all that much?"

"That shouldn't be a problem," Jaclyn said. "What kind of job is it?"

"It's not important," he replied with a bit of hesitation. "What is important is that it will help me take care of Braden. It will also help me get back on my feet."

Jaclyn paused for a few seconds, wanting to ask Sean why he was being so mysterious, but couldn't bring herself to do so. She opened the envelope, removed the check, and placed it in her purse.

"He's going to be excited to see you today," she said. "You're picking him up at 3:30, right?"

"Yep, 3:30 as usual," Sean said, as he nodded. "I've got a few more things to do before then so I better run."

"And remember that his orthodontist appointment is this Friday at 11:45 a.m.," Jaclyn added. "I'm showing property all morning so I still need you to pick him up from school and take him to it, okay?"

"It's on my calendar," Sean said, as he turned slightly toward the door. "I'd better go."

"Okay," replied Jaclyn, as she leaned forward in her chair. "Thanks again for coming by."

Jaclyn rose awkwardly as Sean began to leave, instinctively reaching her arms out to hug him. The gesture surprised him at first, and although he contemplated hugging her as well, he nodded at her instead and left the room.

A few minutes later, Sean found himself sitting in his car in a department store parking lot. He was devouring a sandwich and reading a newspaper. After he finished eating, he folded the paper and placed it in the passenger seat atop a couple of thoroughbred racing magazines that he had recently purchased. He then entered the department store, chewing the last piece of his sandwich as he walked inside.

"Can I help you find something?" asked the young female employee that was stocking shelves in the men's clothing department.

"Yes," Sean said. "I'm looking for some dress shirts."

After picking out a few neckties from a table display, Sean began trying on a series of different shirts in the men's dressing room. He arrived soon after at the checkout counter with a series of neckties draped across his shoulder, as well as a stack of blue dress shirts, all packaged in cellophane. He placed the items on the checkout counter, and the clerk began ringing them up.

"Wow, you must really like blue," the checkout clerk said casually as she sifted through the large stack of blue dress shirts.

"I do," Sean replied.

"Is blue your favorite color?" she inquired, as she began placing the shirts in a bag.

"It is now," Sean answered, with an uneasy smile.

A few minutes later, Sean found himself in the parking lot of an old office park on the north end of town. He was parked outside of the county health department, which occupied one of the offices within the large, white brick building. Nervously, he left his truck and entered the health department, quickly walking past the patients that were waiting in the lobby until he reached the front desk.

"I'm here to take an HIV test," he whispered to the receptionist behind the glass window.

"Okay," said the receptionist, handing Sean a clipboard. "Just fill out this information and bring it back up to me when you're finished."

Sean sat in a flimsy, plastic chair, filling out the paperwork that was attached to the clipboard, occasionally looking around the room at the handful of other people that were doing the same thing. He felt out of place as he looked at the other faces in the room and wondered what brought them there as well. He saw a young couple, apparently married, with three children that were quietly playing nearby. Across the room was an older man sitting with a teenage boy. The older man, possibly the boy's father, looked sad as he stared off into the distance. He saw a female couple holding hands, watching CNN on the television that hung in the corner of the lobby near the doorway. He was self-conscious as he sat there, wondering if anyone there knew him or suspected why he might be there.

Sean was relieved when his name was called, and he was led back to an examination room. A female attendant asked him a few questions, placed a swab in this throat, and placed the saliva sample into a small tube. Sean was confident that he knew what the results of the test would be, since he had spent the last 15 years as a faithful husband to Jaclyn, but it was still nice to hear the attendant tell him that the results were "negative."

"That's good to hear," Sean told her, as he began to put on his coat. He was handed a paper with the test results at the front desk, and then he left the office. Once inside his vehicle, he took a picture of the results with the camera on his cell phone and texted the picture to Anjelica.

"Thank you," texted Anjelica a few minutes later.

That afternoon, he drove to his son's middle school, and sat patiently in his truck while waiting in the parent pickup line. Sean watched as the school children poured out of the front door and into the cars in front of him. The vehicles inched slowly along the driveway before collecting their children and disappearing onto the main road. He then saw Braden, his blonde hair buried in the hood of his winter coat, waving and smiling. He jumped into Sean's truck and they too joined the steady stream of vehicles departing for the day.

"How was school today?" Sean asked.

"Pretty good," Braden replied proudly. "I think I got an 'A' on my social studies test. We won't find out until tomorrow but I did really well on it, I know it."

"Way to go," Sean replied.

"Thanks," Braden said. "Hey Dad, did you lose your job? Mom said that you weren't working anymore."

"I did, Braden," replied Sean, "but it looks like I'm going to be working again soon. It might end up being weekends, so you and your mother are going to have to be patient with me for a while until my schedule gets sorted out, okay?"

"Okay," Braden replied. "Are you still going to be a stockbroker?"

"No, son," Sean answered, as he took a pair of sunglasses off of the dashboard and pushed them over his eyes.

"What is it, then?" asked Braden curiously.

"I guess you could call it the service industry," Sean answered enigmatically.

Later that evening, while Braden did his homework at the kitchen counter, Sean was in the garage. The hum of the vacuum was almost deafening to Sean as he leaned in to sweep out the floorboards of his Suburban. He was meticulous in his cleaning efforts, detailing the vehicle both inside and out, all the while envisioning the passengers who might soon be riding with him. He wondered who they might be, where they might be coming from, and what they would think of him. At one point, he sat in the back seat to get a better view of what they would be seeing. It was a strange vantage point, but it gave him a better idea of what his clients would see. He continued to clean, removing the dust and dirt and boxing up the clutter and putting it on a shelf in the garage. He wanted everything to look perfect, and eventually it did.

After wiping down the leather seats and spraying the carpet with Febreze, he walked around the vehicle one last time. It looked shiny and pristine with its black paint shimmering under the halogen lights of the garage. Sean smiled and went back inside the house.

Later that evening, just before Braden's bedtime, Sean and his son relaxed in the living room. As they watched television, Sean leafed through his thoroughbred magazines. He read several articles, and tried to familiarize himself with much of the terminology in the periodicals.

"Since when do you like horses so much?" asked Braden, as he looked at the magazine in his father's hands.

"Well, I thought that since we are in Kentucky it wouldn't hurt to learn a little bit more about them," Sean replied.

"If you're thinking about getting me a pony for my next birthday - don't," Braden said, as both he and Sean began laughing hysterically.

Eight

Sean hadn't run in years - in fact, he hated jogging, but as he studied himself in his bedroom mirror he noticed a belly that was a little larger than he had remembered it to be. After taking Braden to school that morning, he drove immediately to a nearby park for his first run in what seemed like ages. After a quick sip from his water bottle, he locked his truck and began jogging around the walking track. It was a cold, foggy morning, but he was warm in his black baseball cap and dark gray sweat suit.

As he lumbered along the winding path, he faintly heard the voice of a woman ahead in the distance. Suddenly, he saw a very large dog, a black Labrador retriever, emerging from the wall of fog and approaching fast. At full speed, the dog leapt at Sean, who tried to move quickly out of the way. The dog grazed his side, knocking him down and over into the grass. As he lay there with his back on the grass, the dog began licking his face playfully.

"I'm so sorry," said the woman, who appeared out of nowhere and was now standing directly over Sean. "Major got away from me." Holding a leash, she attached it to the dog's collar and pulled it away from Sean.

"It's all right," Sean said, rising to his feet and dusting off his pants. "He's certainly a friendly guy, isn't he?"

"Friendly is an understatement," she said. "He's so strong sometimes that he gets out of his leash. By the way, I'm Brynn."

"I'm Sean," replied Sean, as he shook her hand and then rubbed his elbow, which was hurting a little from his tumble to the ground.

The woman, who looked to be in her late twenties, was an attractive, petite brunette, wearing a wraparound head scarf, ski vest, blue jeans, and tennis shoes. "Look, I've got to go, but let me make it up to you. Can I buy you a cup of coffee sometime?"

"Sure," Sean answered with a smile.

She gave him her number and then left with her pet. Sean put his cell phone back into his sweat shirt pocket and resumed running. "Did she just ask me out?" he thought to himself. "Maybe this jogging thing isn't so bad after all."

Sweaty and tired, he returned to his truck, stretched his back and legs, and sat on the edge of the driver's seat. He took a long drink from his water bottle, and then he heard a loud beep coming from his phone. Thinking that he had a text, he pulled the phone from the front pouch of his shirt pocket and swiped his finger across the screen. A somewhat subdued smile came across his face as he looked at the phone and saw a large image emblazoned on its screen. It was a symbol with a very simple design - a blue dress shirt and black neck tie. Could this be his first assignment?

Nervously, he swiped the image with his finger, and the graphic dissolved into another screen that resembled a travel itinerary. He noticed a woman's name, a phone number, and below it was some flight information and dates. It was indeed his first assignment with the company. A rush of adrenaline came across his body as he studied the information displayed on the phone. A few moments later, he called Rob.

"Are you home?" Sean asked. "Can I come by for a minute?"

"Sure," Rob replied. "But you'll have to excuse the mess."

Rob's house brought back a lot of memories as Sean walked in the door. Not much had changed, especially in the living room, where Sean sat down on the same couch that had been there twenty years earlier. The house even had the same smell - a clean, fresh scent that reminded Sean of both deodorant and laundry detergent. The walls were still covered with the same cheesy artwork, but what really delighted Sean was the familiar sight of the samurai sword display that was still mounted to the wall.

"Yeah, I still take a lot of shit for those," Rob said, as Sean ran his hand across the blades of the swords. "But they're a great conversation piece. So what brings you by?"

"This," replied Sean, as he turned and handed his phone to Rob.

"Ah, looks like your maiden voyage is fast approaching," Rob said, gliding his finger across the phone and reading the information contained on the screen. "Are you ready?"

"As ready as I can be," Sean responded.

Rob went to his refrigerator and pulled out two bottles of beer, handing one of them to Sean.'"Thornbury', I've never heard of her,"

"What?" asked Sean.

"That's her last name," replied Rob, as he opened his beer. "Most of our clients are repeat customers, but I'm not familiar with that name. Either she's new or she's semi-regular."

"So my first client won't be one of your castoffs?" asked Sean with a sarcastic smile. "What a shame."

"Oh, it'll happen," said Rob. "A lot of the women will use our service 3 or 4 times a year, sometimes more, and most of the time they request different guys. They like variety - it's just how it works."

"Okay," Sean replied, "so it looks like I'm picking her up at the airport on Friday morning at 10:40, does that look right to you?"

"Delta flight, 10:40 a.m. arrival this Friday," muttered Rob, peering into the phone. "That's right. She's flying out at 7:35 a.m. on Monday, so you've got her for 3 days. That's typical. It looks like she's staying downtown at the Hilton. Yep, everything looks pretty straightforward." Rob gave Sean's phone back to him and took a drink of beer.

"So when I pick her up at the airport," Sean inquired, "where do I park? By the terminal where the taxis are?" inquired Sean as he sipped his beer.

"You can," Rob replied, "but it's best to park in short term parking. Some of the flights will be delayed by a few minutes, and you don't want to piss off the taxi drivers and airport security by clogging up the taxi lane during a flight delay. Go to short term parking, then come inside and wait for your client by the luggage return."

"How will she know that I'm her driver?" asked Sean. "Should I hold up a sign with her last name on it?"

"Actually, yes," Rob replied. "She will see the sign that you're holding of course, but she'll also know that it's you because of your blue shirt. Make sure your shirt is visible, even if you're wearing a coat or suit jacket. Anjelica is really into branding, and she loves it when a client meets her driver for this first time and he's in a blue shirt. After that, take her luggage, put her in your car, and then do whatever she asks you to do until you take her back to the airport on Monday morning."

"I withdrew a few hundred bucks so I would have some cash on me this weekend," Sean mentioned. "Do you think that will be enough?"

"Not a bad idea," replied Rob, "but when you're out, your clients are also supposed to pay for everything - dinner, drinks, show tickets, you name it. If you end up buying something for the client, let Anjelica know and she'll take care of reimbursing you for any expenses that you incur. Oh, and you'll need these."

Rob handed Sean a clear sandwich bag filled with yellow pills, which were shaped like small teardrops. Sean studied the contents of the bag briefly and then looked back at Rob.

"What are these?" Sean asked innocently.

"Cialis," Rob replied.

"I'm okay in that department," Sean said, handing the bag back to Rob.

"Trust me," Rob said, pushing the bag away. "You're going to need these. I know right now you don't think that you will, but you will. By the way, did you get your HIV test done?"

"I did, and I already sent it over to Anjelica," Sean replied. "That was a fun experience. It seems kind of weird that a top flight organization like Blue Shirts doesn't have its own in-house doctor for things like that."

"We used to," replied Rob, "He worked for Anjelica for a while, giving us examinations, writing us prescriptions, you name it. Then he went all squirrelly on her. He got arrested for prescription fraud or something like that. He was kind of a shady guy anyway, so it's just as well. Now all the new guys just go to the health department."

"I've got one last question," Sean asked, "has anyone at the company ever been arrested for this? I mean, I know that what we're doing is prostitution. What happens if we get caught? What happens if I get caught?"

"I've never been arrested, and to my knowledge nobody at Blue Shirts has been either," Rob shared. "Rest assured, Anjelica has all of the bases covered. Her screening process is very thorough, and she has her clients sign a waiver that states that we are providing them with transportation services only. The companionship that we provide outside of that agreement is complimentary, therefore it's not illegal."

"What if someone with a badge doesn't see it that way?" Sean inquired.

"Look Sean," Rob continued, "this isn't street corner stuff. The local PD doesn't know about us, and even if they did they wouldn't care. It's a class B misdemeanor - so if any of us got caught, absolute worst case scenario we'd get a slap on the wrist and we'd be on our merry way."

"I guess that makes me feel a little better," Sean replied, as he finished his beer.

"Good," Rob said. "Now let's get some lunch, I'm starving."

Nine

There wasn't much activity at Bluegrass Airport on Friday morning, which was a relief to Sean as he pulled into the taxi lane. His black Suburban looked a bit out of place behind the yellow taxicabs that were parked in front of him, but he was more concerned about his own appearance as he removed his sunglasses, adjusted his hair, and took one last look at his cell phone. He stared for a few moments at the last text he received the night before, in which Jaclyn confirmed that she could keep Braden this weekend. He thought of his son, took a deep breath, exited his truck and walked into the airport.

His stomach was churning as he walked towards the baggage claim. He stood out from most everyone else in the sparse crowd with his blue dress shirt and black dress slacks, as the few people in the terminal were dressed much more casually. As he made his way through the airport lobby, he passed an older man and woman holding hands, as well as a young man wearing a sports jersey and listening to music on a set of headphones. Sean also noticed an African-American man in a blue jumpsuit, wearing a baseball cap and holding a walkie-talkie. The man looked like an employee of one of the airlines, perhaps a technician, as he was wearing a lanyard that had the name of the airport on it. As the men passed each other, Sean made eye contact with the man in the jumpsuit, and then saw him whisper into his walkie-talkie. Sean thought it was strange, but he continued walking toward the luggage carousel.

Standing alone near the carousel, Sean confirmed with several glances at his phone that he was about 20 minutes early. In his left hand he nervously held a white sheet of paper with the name 'Thornbury' scrawled on it, and he wondered if he would be able to hold up the sign without his client seeing his hands shaking.

He looked again at his phone, rechecking his client's arrival time. As he raised his head up, he noticed that he was no longer alone - as another man was standing just a few feet away from him. The man, who had a scruffy beard and was wearing a red shirt and khaki pants, was looking around the room anxiously. He looked at Sean, and then looked away quickly.

A few seconds later, Sean glanced across the carousel and saw two other men, both dressed in blue jumpsuits like the man he saw a few minutes earlier. They looked at Sean and then started scurrying about after they caught him staring at them. Already nervous, Sean glanced over his shoulder and was met with a sight that made his blood run cold - it was an older man in a gray trench coat striding towards him. The man, who was thin and had short, gray hair, was wearing a shiny badge around his neck and holding a gun in his right hand. Sean then glanced to his right and saw the two men in jumpsuits charging towards him as well, each of them brandishing handguns as well.

Sean was almost sick with emotion - he knew instantly that these men were police officers, and he knew that he was going to be arrested. His thoughts were racing just as fast as his pulse as he wondered what he would tell his son, his parents - even Jaclyn. Without hesitation, Sean dropped his sign, raised his hands and placed them on the back of his head, ready to surrender to the men and accept the consequences that would soon be at hand.

To Sean's surprise, the three men, plus the man he had seen a few minutes earlier who was also wearing a blue jumpsuit, raced past him and tackled the man next to him. As Sean stood there with his hands behind his head, he watched as the men arrested the scruffy man, who was now lying prone on the carpet. The men in jumpsuits, who were apparently undercover police officers, arrested the man and began reading him his rights. "We got him," said the older man in the trench coat, as he looked at his fellow officers excitedly. The men in jumpsuits led the scruffy man outside to a waiting police car. Sean stood frozen, still holding his hands behind his head with his fingers interlaced.

"You okay, sir?" asked the older man. "You can put your hands down if you like."

"I'm okay," Sean replied. "What happened?"

"That guy's bad news," the man said. "He's one of the biggest drug dealers in the southeast. We've been tracking him for weeks but now we've got him."

"That's good to know," Sean said.

"By the way, I'm Detective Wyatt," the man said, handing Sean a business card. "I'm an officer with the Lexington Police Department. We might need to get a witness statement from you in a few days. Could I get your name and contact information if we need to bring you to the station to answer a few questions? It's just procedure, you know."

"Sure, that'd be fine," replied Sean, as the color returned to his face. He gave the man his name and phone number.

"Thanks," replied the Detective. "I'll be in touch." He bent down and picked up the sign that was on the carpet, looked at it, and handed it to Sean. "Is this yours?"

"Yes, thank you," Sean replied.

"You a limo driver?" asked the Detective.

"Sort of," Sean said, "I'm a chauffer."

"I see," replied the Detective. "I didn't see a limo outside, what are you driving?"

"A Suburban," Sean replied. "It's in the parking lot."

Detective Wyatt looked at Sean, somewhat puzzled, then nodded and left. Sean stood alone by the luggage carousel, with the handful of people who had watched the commotion from afar beginning to disperse. Suddenly a loud buzz filled the room as the carousel began to move, slowly filling with suitcases. Sean took a deep breath, put the business card in his wallet, and held the sign up to his chest. He watched as a group of people descended from a nearby escalator and gathered around the carousel. Sean watched the various men and women as they pulled their luggage from the conveyer, trying to put the events of the last few minutes behind him and focus on his task at hand. He forced a smile as he peered into the crowd of people, wondering who among them might be his client. One by one they walked by him on their way out of the airport, with Sean examining each one as they passed by him. Nearly everyone had left except for a woman, who was fidgeting with her luggage as she approached him.

"Hello, I'm Stella Thornbury," the woman said with a warm smile and thick New York accent. "You must be my driver."

"It's my pleasure," Sean replied, taking her luggage. "My name is Sean, it's very good to meet you, Ms. Thornbury."

"Please, call me Stella," she said, as the pair began walking outside towards Sean's truck. "You'll have to excuse me if I seem on edge - I get nervous when I fly so I'm a little hyper right now."

"That's quite all right," Sean replied, as the pair walked to his vehicle. The woman, who appeared to be in her late fifties, had short, bobbed blonde hair, and was wearing an unbuttoned black coat that revealed a colorful, leopard-print blouse. She also sported an abundance of jewelry, including several gold bracelets and rings and diamond earrings that dangled from her ears.

Sean loaded her suitcase into the back of the truck and opened the rear passenger door. Stella thanked him, removed her coat, and stepped out of the chilly morning air and into the vehicle.

"Where are you staying?" Sean inquired.

"I'm staying downtown at the Hilton," she replied. "But my check-in isn't until this afternoon. Can you take me around the city before we go to the hotel? I haven't been here in years and would love to take in all of the sights."

"Certainly," Sean replied.

Stella took her cell phone from the pocket of her coat and made a call as Sean drove them out of the airport. As she was talking, he began to feel a sense of relief. He was still reeling from witnessing the drug bust earlier that morning, but he was starting to feel at ease now that he had met his client. After the close call with the authorities, having a stranger in his back seat - especially one who was renting him for the next three days - didn't seem as awkward as he had imagined it would be.

"So what brings you to town?" asked Sean, after he saw that Stella had wrapped up her phone conversation.

"Oh, I just adore Kentucky," Stella replied in a thick, New York accent. "I'm a lifelong New Yorker - from Long Island originally - but I used to come to Lexington with my husband years ago. He would buy horses here and take them back up to New York to race at Saratoga."

"I see," Sean replied. "So you must love horses."

"I adore them," she said. "My husband did too. He was in the horse business, I was in show business. We were a perfect match I guess you could say."

"What kind of show business?" Sean asked.

"I'm an actress," Stella replied. "or you could say that I was an actress, depending on how you look at it. I did a lot of theatre, some television too. Are you old enough to remember The Love Boat? I did a guest spot on there once, as well as Fantasy Island, The Rockford Files, and a few other shows."

"I remember those shows," Sean replied with a nostalgic smile. "So you were a pretty big deal then, huh?"

"Well, I wouldn't say that," Stella said. "But it was fun. My first love has always been the theatre though - musical theatre especially. I started out on Broadway, and then moved to L.A. to do film and TV. It was fun, but after a couple of years I decided to move back to New York and start doing theatre again - that's when I met my husband. He traveled a lot in his line of work, and when I didn't have a show I'd tag along with him. We had so much fun on our trips to Kentucky, especially visiting the farms and seeing the countryside. I'm very much a people person, and you have the nicest people here too - so friendly. You don't find a lot of nice people in New York City, at least nowadays."

"Is that where live now?" asked Sean.

"Yes," answered Stella, "we have an apartment in Manhattan. Have you ever been to New York City?"

"No, but I've always wanted to go," Sean replied. "So are you still married?"

"Yes, still married," Stella replied. "It will be 34 years this July. Can you believe it? 34 years. We have a son, his name is Clay. He's 28 and is in L.A. trying to be an actor too - I guess he takes after me more than his father."

Stella laughed, and so did Sean, although his mind was elsewhere. As he navigated through traffic along New Circle Road, he was thinking about Stella's marital situation. He knew that eventually he would probably encounter a married woman while working with the company, but he didn't imagine that his very first client would be married. He wondered if her husband knew what she was doing, or more importantly, what she was likely about to do. He felt a little guilty that she was probably going to be committing adultery with him this weekend, but he knew that this was all part of the job.

While amidst this crisis of conscience, Sean's cell phone began beeping. He glanced down and saw a message on his calendar reminding him about his son's orthodontist appointment. He had forgotten the appointment, which was taking place in 30 minutes. His mind raced as he scrambled for options - should he call the orthodontist and try to reschedule, or perhaps just ignore the appointment altogether and endure Jaclyn's wrath? Sean was a responsible parent, and he knew that Braden was looking forward to seeing him today and getting to leave school for a little while in the process. Could he drop Stella off somewhere, perhaps her hotel, and still pick Braden up from school and take him to his appointment? He weighed each option briefly yet thoroughly, but still couldn't decide what to do.

"What was that?" asked Stella. "If that was a text you can take it, I don't mind."

"I was supposed to pick up my son from school in a few minutes and take him to an appointment," Sean said. "I forgot about it, so I'll probably call them in a few minutes and reschedule if that's okay."

"Nonsense!" shouted Stella gleefully. "A parent is the most important thing you can be. How far away is his school?

"It's just a couple of miles away actually," Sean replied, "but really it's okay."

"Let's go there right now and get him," Stella said. "Besides, I'd love to meet him. How old is he?"

"He's 12," Sean replied hesitantly. "Are you sure?"

"I insist," she replied.

"I really appreciate this," Sean said. "I know this is probably the last thing that you wanted to do once you came into town, but..."

"Quite the contrary," Stella interrupted. "I love children, and I miss the days when my son was your son's age. This is a wonderful surprise - I should be thanking you for allowing me to tag along."

Surprised, Sean navigated through traffic and arrived at Braden's school a few minutes later. He was relieved that he would be able to follow through with the appointment, but began to wonder how he would explain to Braden about the strange lady in the backseat of the truck who would be accompanying them to the orthodontist. Sean parked in the parent pickup area and began to exit his vehicle.

"I'll be right back, Stella," Sean said. "Just wait right here and I'll be back shortly."

"Nonsense," she replied as she exited the vehicle. "I'm coming with you."

"Really?" asked Sean. "You don't have to, it's fine."

"I miss these days terribly," Stella said, "I haven't been inside a school in years and would love to roam the hallways one more time!"

Nervously, Sean held the school's front door open for Stella as the pair entered the lobby. Sean approached Mrs. Tingley, the front desk receptionist, with

Stella closely behind him.

"Oh my word," Stella said loudly as she looked around the lobby, "I simply adore it!"

Sean smiled, a bit embarrassed. "I'm here to pick up Braden Everett."

"Certainly," said Mrs. Tingley, handing Sean a clipboard and pen. "Just sign here. Would you like me to send for him or would you like to go to his classroom and get him?"

"You can send for him," Sean responded.

"I won't hear of it," said Stella to Sean. "We'll go to his classroom," she said to Mrs. Tingley, who nodded confusingly and handed her a small wicker basket filled with visitors stickers. Stella took two of the stickers, placing one on her blouse and one on Sean's shirt. As Stella flattened the sticker onto his shirt, Sean looked at Mrs. Tingley, smiled nervously, then proceeded to leave the lobby with Stella.

Moments later, the unlikely pair was outside of Braden's classroom. Sean knocked on the door, and Braden's teacher, Mrs. Faulkner, answered.

"I'm here for Braden," Sean said.

"Oh, come in," said Mrs. Faulkner as she ushered Sean and Stella into the room. "Braden, your father is here to get you."

As his son walked towards him, Sean introduced Stella to Braden's teacher.

"Mrs. Faulkner, this is my, uh - friend, Stella," Sean said clumsily.

"It's a pleasure," Stella said, shaking hands with Mrs. Faulkner. "I love your classroom - oh, it brings back so many memories."

"Thank you," Mrs. Faulkner said. "Were you a teacher?"

"I wasn't," replied Stella, "but I loved school when I was a child. I also have a grown son and I have so many wonderful memories when he was this age. You must really love what you do."

"I do," said Mrs. Faulkner, gushing with energy.

"Well, we have to be going," Sean said. He patted Braden's back and began the journey back through the hallway. Braden restrained his confusion as best as he could as he wondered who this woman was and why she was with his father.

"You're certainly a handsome young man," Stella said to Braden as she entered the back seat of the Suburban.

Braden, sitting in the front passenger seat next to his father, thanked her for the compliment. They exited the school and made the short drive to the office park where the orthodontist was located. Once there, Stella joined Sean and Braden inside the office and sat with Sean in the lobby while Braden was being examined in an adjacent room. Sean nervously darted his eyes around the room. He watched the young women working behind the counter as they were checking patients in and out. He fidgeted slightly in his chair as he looked across the lobby at the other patients and their families, and observed them as they checked their cell phones. Sean was growing increasing paranoid that someone there would recognize him and wonder who Stella might be. Just then, Sean saw a young girl in a white dress sitting across the room staring at him. As he looked back at her, she smiled at him, proudly showing off a colorful set of red metal braces that were wrapped around her teeth.

"She's cute, isn't she?" asked Stella, as she placed her hand in Sean's hand.

"She definitely is," Sean replied.

"I desperately wanted braces when I was her age," Stella continued. "My teeth were straight for the most part, but I loved the way that they sparkled and shined on my classmates that were fortunate enough to have them. Like most families back then, my parents couldn't afford them, but that didn't stop me from pestering them about getting them for me. So after my acting career was over, I decided to get them. I still didn't need them, but my childhood longing for them never really went away."

"Braden definitely doesn't share your passion for orthodontics," said Sean, as he tried to relax in his chair. "He's here because he needs them, because unfortunately he inherited his father's teeth."

"Well, braces are expensive, Sean," added Stella, "and Braden is lucky to have a father who is not only a good provider, but who also loves him enough to see that he gets everything he needs. I admire that in you."

Stella squeezed Sean's hand as they smiled at each other.

Ten

It was early Friday evening, and Detective Tom Wyatt had just entered his favorite Irish bar when he was greeted with a loud "Surprise!" from the police officers that had gathered inside the tavern. Wyatt was caught off guard, but he smiled, nodded, shook hands, and made his way across the bar to an open seat that was waiting for him. Bouncing into helium-filled balloons and getting tangled occasionally in a streamer, he glided onto an empty barstool next to Detective Abby Miles.

"Surprised?" asked Abby, as she pushed a cold mug of Guinness beer towards him.

"Very surprised, considering my birthday still isn't for a couple of weeks," Detective Wyatt responded as he took a drink of the beer. "So who's behind this anyway, as if I even need to ask?" he inquired with a wry smile on his face.

"Okay, okay," Abby replied, "I might have had a little something to do with the planning, but you only turn 60 once."

"Youth is full of sport, age's breath is short," said Wyatt, smiling wistfully as he tilted back his mug for another drink of beer.

"Ah, I know I'm in for a long night when you start quoting Shakespeare," replied Abby as a couple of fellow officers passed by Wyatt and patted him on the back. "Most cops your age would have retired by now, but you're still here. Are you just bored, stupid or crazy?"

"All of the above," Wyatt responded, loosening his tie and taking another drink of beer.

Tom Wyatt was a well-respected detective, and had a reputation as one of the most brilliant men at the Lexington Police Department. Originally from Cincinnati, his family moved to Lexington in the 1960s. His father, Richard "Buckeye" Wyatt, was a prominent lawyer in the city for several years before being elected as Lexington's District Attorney in the 1970s. At the time, Tom was taking criminal justice classes at Eastern Kentucky University, about a half hour south of Lexington in Richmond. A gifted athlete, Tom received a baseball scholarship, and also became a varsity letterman on both the basketball and track teams. Tom was also brilliant academically, excelling especially in English literature, which blossomed into enough of a passion that he seriously considered becoming an English professor after graduation rather than a police officer. However Wyatt's father, bolstered by his recent political success, urged him to pursue a career in law enforcement, so he enrolled at the police academy and became an officer in 1977. Wyatt married his college sweetheart the following year, and after purchasing a home in a neighborhood on Lexington's east side, they had two sons.

Wyatt spent the first part of his career as a homicide detective, but the long hours began to put a strain on his marriage. He found that dealing with murderers on a day-to-day basis had begun to depress him. Working homicide affected Wyatt on many levels - from the stomach-churning reality of standing over a lifeless victim to the addictive challenge of getting inside the minds of the people that committed these atrocities. After slightly more than a decade in homicide, Wyatt was transferred to the "special enforcement division" at the department.

The special enforcement division consisted of three departments - narcotics, alcohol beverage control, and vice. Like many cities its size, drugs had been a constant issue over the years in Lexington, so the narcotics department was well-staffed with a team of officers dedicated to "cleaning up the streets." The A.B.C. had far less activity than narcotics, as well as a smaller staff. The officers in this department spent most of their time watching the college bars, making sure that the under-21 crowd didn't filter in from campus to try and buy alcohol. By far and away, the department with the least amount of activity was the vice squad. It had become somewhat of an afterthought in the city, as the two primary crimes it investigated - illegal gambling and prostitution - had both become almost nonexistent in Lexington over the last several years.

Gambling hadn't been a problem in the city for quite some time, especially now that it was so easily accessible to people who lived in and around the city. It could be done legally in Lexington at Keeneland and The Red Mile, the city's two horse racing tracks, both of which allowed legal wagering almost year-round. Over the last 20 years, casinos began to spring up in southern Indiana and Ohio, which were a short 90-minute drive. Just about every gas station in the state sold lottery tickets, and thanks to cellular technology and the internet, you could gamble online on almost anything and never have to leave the house.

Prostitution in Lexington still existed to a small degree, but it was essentially wiped out in the late 1990s when the department shut down the massage parlors that had been operating throughout the city. These businesses, most of which were Asian-owned and had names like "Osaka Health Spa" and "Golden Wind Health Spa", were actually 'fronts' for prostitution. Detective Wyatt, along with a team of younger officers, took part in two of the sting operations that brought down these illicit businesses, which led to the arrests, convictions, and deportations of virtually every woman who had been employed at these establishments. Aside from a couple of escort services that continued to advertise in the local Yellow Pages, prostitution was practically unheard of in Lexington, so much so that the city's vice squad consisted of only two detectives - Tom Wyatt and Abby Miles.

Abby was tall and beautiful, with dark, shoulder-length auburn hair and a fair complexion. She was in her late forties, and had been a police officer for the last twenty years. Originally from Bowling Green, Kentucky, she moved to Lexington to attend college at the University of Kentucky. After graduating in 1990 with a degree in communications, she began an internship at one of the local television stations. She spent a few months as an on-air reporter, and with her combination of beauty, intelligence, and tenacity, it seemed like only a matter of time before she would ascend to an anchor position. Things began to unravel when she began an affair with the station's charismatic weatherman, who was handsome, charming, popular, and also married. Although it lasted just a few weeks, Abby soon discovered that she was pregnant. Although she had fallen in love with the weatherman, the feelings were unrequited, and he made it clear to her that he couldn't leave his wife for her. Rather than face the indignity of seeing her former lover at work each day for the foreseeable future, Abby chose to abandon her career in television news to focus on being a mother. A short time later her daughter was born, whom she named Alyssa. As a single parent, Abby worked at a variety of jobs for the next few months to make ends meet before deciding to become a police officer.

As a young cadet at the police academy, she met Detective Wyatt, who took her under his wing, mentoring her and helping shape her into becoming a good officer. She had worked as a patrol officer for six years at the department but transferred to the vice squad when that position became available. She found that being a vice detective fit her schedule with Alyssa better, allowing her to spend much more time with her daughter. She also jumped at the chance to work with Wyatt, a man that she had always respected and admired. Over the years, they hadn't worked many vice cases together, but they were both frequently being asked to help their fellow officers in narcotics with investigations, stings, and the occasional arrest.

"How did your bust at the airport go today?" asked Abby, as she crossed her legs and pulled a pretzel out of the small bowl resting on the bar.

"It was good," said Wyatt, "although there was something odd about it."

"Odd?" Abby asked.

"Yeah," continued Wyatt. "When we closed in to make the arrest, there was a guy standing by the suspect that saw me coming and put his hands behind his head."

"Did he know the suspect?" asked Abby.

"I don't believe so," Wyatt said. "But there was a look in his eye - a look of guilt. It's as if he knew he was doing something wrong and that I was there to arrest him instead of the perpetrator."

"Did you run a check on him yet?" Abby asked. "Maybe he has a warrant."

"I did a preliminary check on him," Wyatt continued. "No warrants, no criminal history, just a few speeding tickets. Looks like he's clean, but I still have this feeling about him that I can't quite put my finger on."

"Then it sounds like it's nothing to worry about," Abby said. "If it will make you feel better, I'll do a little digging on him this weekend and see what I can find.

"I appreciate it but you don't have to," said Wyatt.

"No, I insist," Abby replied. "What's his name?"

"Sean Everett," Wyatt said begrudgingly.

"Okay, I'll see what I can find," Abby said. "But for now, just sit back, relax, and enjoy your party."

Just then, the server brought out a large birthday cake, complete with several candles, and put it on the bar between Detective Wyatt and Abby. As his fellow officers gathered around him to serenade him with a chorus of "Happy Birthday", he smiled at Abby and blew out the candles.

Not far from the bar, Sean was in a hotel suite at the Hilton, staring into the bathroom mirror and tightening his necktie. Stella, who was sitting on the bed putting on her shoes, was now wearing a beautiful yellow dress. While sipping from a glass of vodka and cranberry juice, she wrapped up a conversation on her cell phone. It was almost 6 o'clock, and they would be leaving for dinner soon.

Sean was impressed with the suite, with its bedroom, living room, kitchenette and bathroom, which featured an enormous garden tub. He stood beside the circular tub, which was covered in beige tiles, and marveled at the many Jacuzzi jets that lined its beige interior. He then wandered over to the table near the window, opening the small suitcase that he had placed next to Stella's larger suitcase. He pulled out a different tie from the suitcase and held it up to his chest, comparing it to the one he was already wearing. After closing his suitcase, he looked out the window and saw the high rise office building that he had worked inside for the last few years.

"What a difference a week makes," he muttered to himself, realizing that it had been seven days since his departure from the brokerage firm. He thought of the changes his life had undergone since his dismissal. Last week he was a stockbroker, anchored to a desk and watching numbers most of the day. Now he was something radically different - a gigolo - a man who was being paid to do very different things than what he did in his previous career.

As he watched Stella finish getting ready, Sean ran a lint roller across his black pants and returned to the bathroom. Looking in the mirror, he removed the tie that he was wearing and started to put the new one on when Stella's reflection appeared.

"Let me help you with that," she said, entering the bathroom and turning his shoulders around to face her. She slowly tightened the necktie into a Windsor knot, then took the tie, pulling Sean closer to her own body. She closed her eyes, moved closer to his face, and kissed him on the mouth. During the kiss, Sean opened his eyes for a moment - surprised at first that this was happening - and looked at Stella as she pulled herself closer into his arms. He then closed his eyes and kissed her back, pulling her closer to his body as well.

Thirty minutes later, they were sitting in a quaint, yet fancy restaurant not far from the hotel. Stella ordered the Chilean sea bass and a glass of wine, while Sean ordered the swordfish entree. Stella nibbled on her salad while Sean took a roll from the basket on the table. He looked around the half-filled restaurant wondering if there was anyone there he knew. He felt a bit more at ease at the hotel when it was just he and Stella, but some of the nervousness that he experienced earlier in the day at Braden's school had returned.

"I've felt like all I've done today is talk about me," Stella said, caressing her glass of Chardonnay. "Tell me more about you, Sean."

"There's not much to tell, really," he responded.

"Are you from here?" she asked.

"Born and raised," Sean replied.

"Married or divorced?" Stella inquired.

"Recently divorced," Sean said, taking a gulp of his drink. "She's a real estate agent here in town. Braden is our only child - we have joint custody, but she gets him a little more than I do."

"I see," Stella said, circling the top of her wine glass with her finger. "What was your previous profession before you joined the oldest profession?"

They both laughed, and Sean began to feel much more comfortable. "I was a stockbroker," he answered. "I worked just across the street actually. I've always been a numbers guy - was good at math in school, studied marketing in college. I loved my job, and was really good at it. But things change, and a few days ago they let me know that my services were no longer required. The next day, an old friend of mine told me about Blue Shirts, and here I am."

"So I'm your first?" she asked, as she smiled and took another sip of her wine.

"That you are," Sean replied, smiling from ear to ear. "So be gentle."

"I can't make any promises," Stella responded, laughing almost hysterically while Sean shook his head and smiled.

"Well, I hope that I don't disappoint you," said Sean, as he took another drink.

"Oh, I'm easy to please, just ask Anjelica," Stella replied. "I've been coming to Lexington by myself for ten years or more. Arthur - that's my husband - doesn't like to travel, but I don't mind it at all. It's the loneliness that I'm not particularly fond of, so when I'm visiting somewhere I prefer having a companion. Sure, I like the safety of having a man around when I'm in town, but it's the company that I prefer. Experiences are much more fun and interesting when they're shared, don't you agree?"

"I do," Sean replied, taking a piece of bread from the basket on the table.

"I tried to enjoy myself during my first few trips here without Arthur, but it just wasn't the same," Stella continued. "That's when I was referred to Anjelica. I've used her service ever since."

"Have you ever met her?" Sean asked.

"Why yes," Stella replied, "I've been to her home on several occasions. I usually try to stop by and visit her each time I come to the city. She's hosting a party at her home tomorrow night, and I told her that we would attend."

"Fantastic," said Sean with a raised eyebrow.

As their entrees arrived, Sean enjoyed listening to Stella's stories of thoroughbred horses, show business, and New York high society. Stella also spoke of Lexington's high society, and how many years ago she and her husband dabbled in that scene as well. She reminisced about the grand parties she attended in Lexington during the 1970s, and how she "rubbed elbows" at these events with celebrities from the worlds of movies, television, and sports. Sean was both amused and fascinated by these stories, but was especially drawn to the darker details of the parties, which Stella would allude to but never actually describe. She hinted frequently about the debauchery that she witnessed while attending these parties, but was too much of a lady to recount them at the dinner table to Sean.

After finishing dinner, they left the restaurant and began walking down the sidewalk, stopping into an occasional bar for a drink. By night's end, they were back at the hotel, and Stella was drunk. With Sean's help, she undressed and then fell backwards onto the bed, laughing and mumbling. Sean placed the covers over her and crawled into the bed beside her. He began to kiss her, but he quickly realized that she had passed out. He smiled, put his arm around her, and fell asleep beside her.

Eleven

Sean and Stella spent Saturday afternoon driving around Lexington. Although she had visited as recently as last year, she marveled at the changing landscape of the city. He drove her into the wooded roads that wound themselves outside of the city and into the countryside, passing the horse farms and elegant mansions that were sprawled across the landscape. It was warm again, and the grass looked much greener than it had in previous weeks. Spring would be here very soon.

They arrived at Anjelica's house later that evening, which looked much different to Sean compared to his previous visit. Her street was overrun with black SUVs - Suburbans, Escalades, Navigators, as far as the eye could see. Some of the vehicles were parked in her driveway, but most of them were parked along the street. As they approached her front door, a man in a black suit escorted them inside and took their coats. There was music and chatter coming from the rear of the house, so Stella led Sean to the living room.

As they entered the room, Sean was taken aback by everything he saw. There were several women, maybe a dozen or so, dressed in evening gowns and cocktail dresses. There were also around a dozen men, all of whom were wearing blue dress shirts and black slacks, mingling with the women. Lively music filled the air, as did loud and lively conversation. Many of the guests had paired off into couples and were scattered throughout the room. Just a few feet away, Sean saw a couple who was dancing rather gracefully. They said hello to him and Stella just prior to completing a twirl and dip that brought cheers from several of the other guests. To his right, Sean saw a few of the men sitting on the couches, with their dates draped over them. A few of the men were holding cigars, and a slight cloud of smoke hovered over the couches. Sean looked at the couples, and he watched as these women shot long, flirtatious looks towards him. He noticed Samson, the man he had met at Anjelica's house during his first visit, relaxing on the couch with a lady sitting on his lap. Samson winked at Sean, and then continued to converse with the woman who was perched upon his leg.

In another corner of the room, Sean saw Rob, who was embracing a woman with short, gray hair. As she kissed him, Rob looked at Sean and raised his glass to him. Just then, Anjelica appeared through the doorway, and entered the room holding a tray of hors d'oeurves. One of the men took the tray from her as she smiled and rushed over to Stella to greet her.

"Stella, my dear, it's so good to see you," Anjelica said as she hugged her. "How was your trip?"

"It was marvelous," Stella answered. "I'm having the best time, and I have this young man to thank."

"It's I who should be thanking you," Sean replied to Stella, before turning to Anjelica. "Stella is absolutely amazing."

"She certainly is," said Anjelica. "Stella, please come in and enjoy yourself. One of my boys will be happy to get you a drink, and feel free to help yourself to anything that you see. I need to steal Sean away for a moment if that's okay, but I'll have him back to you before you know it."

"That's quite all right," said Stella, as one of the men handed her a drink, took her hand, and led her into the party.

"We need to talk," Anjelica whispered to Sean, taking his hand and leading him down a hallway and into a small study. When she shut the door, Sean was surprised to see Rob waiting in the room as well.

"She looks like she's having a good time," Rob said. "Are you?"

"It's going really well," Sean responded, sidestepping Rob's question. "Isn't it?" he asked, looking somewhat meekly at Anjelica.

"Stella has been a client of mine for years, and I don't know if I've ever seen her looking so happy as she does tonight," said Anjelica. "You're obviously doing something right. But she isn't the reason why I called you in here. You see, Sean, I have a problem and I need your help."

"Sure, anything I can do to help," replied Sean. "What is it?"

"Periodically, I have clients come to me with unusual requests," she continued, "and I pride myself on my ability to fulfill these requests, no matter how difficult they might be. One of my oldest and dearest clients is arriving Monday night, and she is in need of an Asian man. Unfortunately, I don't have any Asian men on staff here at the company, and my efforts this week to find one have proven unsuccessful."

"You want me to find an Asian guy for Blue Shirts?" asked Sean. "Isn't recruitment more of Rob's responsibility?"

"I've looked high and low and can't find anyone," Rob said, "especially someone that we can trust."

"I'm sorry," said Sean, "I don't really have any Asian friends, or know anyone of Asian descent to tell you the truth."

"Really?," asked Anjelica. "They can be Chinese, Japanese, Korean. It's very important that we find someone for her, someone who's a team player like you and Rob. Next month is going to be very busy for us, so we can likely keep him on permanently if he so desires."

"I wish I could help," Sean said, "I don't really know of anyone except, well..."

"I knew it!" Rob exclaimed. "I knew my Sean wouldn't let us down. Who is it?"

"Well, I don't really know him," Sean continued. "The last couple of years I've been grabbing lunch at a Chinese restaurant on the west end of town. It isn't that far from my old office, so most of the time my co-workers would come with me.

Every time we ate there, I saw a Chinese guy sitting in the corner of the restaurant. Sometimes the girls that worked there would come over and sit with him and talk to him. Other times he would sit alone - always with a laptop on the table and his cell phone in his hand."

"Did you ever talk to him?" asked Anjelica. "What's his name?"

"I don't know his name," Sean responded. "And I've never had a conversation with him. But I'm sure that the woman who owns the restaurant knows him, and I've talked with her a few times. She's really friendly, so I can probably get her to introduce me to him."

"How old is he?" asked Rob. "Is he Blue Shirt material?"

"I can't tell if he's 30 or 13," Sean replied. "He's got spiky hair, and dresses with a kind of hip hop style. Other than that, he's in good shape and is a pretty decent looking guy."

"Well, beggars can't be choosers now, can they?" asked Rob sarcastically.

"He's literally the only person I can think of," Sean said. "At the very least, if he's not interested maybe he knows someone who would be."

"Rest assured, this isn't normally how we do things," said Anjelica. "We rarely hire at the company, and when we do it is only through a referral from another Blue Shirt. Obviously, recruitment at our company is a delicate matter, and secrecy is essential. Choose your words carefully with this fellow, as we don't want to draw any unwanted attention to us should he decline our invitation."

"If he says 'no', what then?" Sean asked. "I would imagine the last thing that you want is someone out there knowing about us. What if he tells someone? What if he tells the police?"

"Fortunately, that's never happened," Anjelica answered. "We don't recruit someone unless we know that their answer is going to be 'yes'."

"Like we did with you, old boy," Rob added, as he smiled and raised his glass to Sean.

"This situation is different," continued Anjelica. "Feel him out first to see if he's interested, and then use your discretion throughout the conversation to see if he's amenable to our offer. Be subtle - drop a hint or two here and there, but don't just blurt out that we're an escort agency or anything like that. You'll know if things are going well, and then at that point you can share more information with him. If he declines, then you are to call me immediately, at which point I'll send Samson over to talk to him. Samson will convey to him just how much harm would come to him and his family should he decide to tell anyone about his conversation with you. He may seem like a big teddy bear, but Samson can be very persuasive."

"I understand," Sean replied, "and will do my best. When does the client arrive?"

"Her flight arrives Monday at 7:15 p.m.," Anjelica responded. "Stella leaves that morning, so after you take her to the airport you'll need to go to the restaurant and see if your friend is there. If he agrees to join us, I'll need you to bring him here immediately after you meet with him so I can set him up in our system. That afternoon we'll take care of his dress clothes, vehicle, and other details."

"If he says no," Sean said, "what's your backup plan?"

"There is no backup plan," Anjelica replied. "I'm confident that you'll be able to take care of this matter."

Sean left the room with Anjelica and Rob and returned to the party. Stella was dancing in the middle of the room with some of the other guests, and beckoned for Sean to join her. As he danced with Stella, Sean continued to glance around the room, and watched as the women talked, flirted and danced with their dates. He was mesmerized by the sights, and his mind raced with many thoughts. He looked at many of the other men in the room, all gigolos like himself, and wondered what roads might have led them to this strange existence. The men, most of whom were athletic in build and ranged in age between 30 and 50, seemed to genuinely enjoy the attention that their clients were bestowing upon them. The ladies, most of whom were in their 50s and 60s, were dancing, drinking, giggling and flirting with the men who were scattered about the room.

As he continued to survey the room, Sean found himself pleasantly surprised at how beautiful many of the women were. Like most men, he had a penchant for attractive women, and he was relieved to see so many of them gathered in the room.

As Sean spun Stella on the expensive Oriental rug that had become a makeshift dance floor, he absorbed his surroundings. He realized that the house wasn't just Anjelica's home, but it was also her place of business, at least for tonight. Although he had never set foot in a bordello, he grew to accept that he was now inside one. But this was no ordinary whorehouse - yes, there was Anjelica, a sociable, charismatic, madam who cavorted throughout the home with an uncanny ease. And yes, her house had an old world feel, as if it were from a different era entirely, with its portraits of Belle Brezing, furniture, and other assorted memorabilia. But the startling difference, and most noticeable of all, was the role reversal of the genders. The women, not the men, held all of the power in the room. They had all of the control, all of the money, and all of the power. The men in the room were there to serve the women - nothing more, nothing less - in whatever capacity was seen fit.

Throughout the evening, Anjelica introduced Sean to almost all of the women at the party, as well as many of the Blue Shirts. There was Derek, who was the oldest gentleman there. With shoulder-length, flowing gray hair, Derek was a ruggedly handsome man with movie star good looks. He told Sean that he had been with the company for nearly ten years, and that he lived in Las Vegas but commuted to Lexington frequently in order to entertain clients for the company.

"Do you like Vegas?" Derek asked. "Look me up if you're ever out there."

Sean nodded as Derek handed him a business card. Stella introduced Sean to Raoul, a Hispanic man in his early 40s with wavy black hair. While Stella was in the kitchen talking with some of the other ladies, Raoul told Sean that he was originally from Mexico, and that he used to own a restaurant in Guadalajara but he sold it and moved here to work for Anjelica. He had been a Blue Shirt for six years, and also happened to be Stella's companion when she came to Lexington last spring.

"Such a sweet lady," Raoul shared. "I could listen to her stories all day long."

Rob introduced Sean to Colby, who looked a little different from the rest of the men. In his mid 40s, Colby had a shaved head and a slight paunch that protruded from his stomach and pressed tightly against the buttons of his dark blue shirt.

"Colby was my last recruit before you," Rob said to Sean, while patting Colby on the back. "I've known him since our car selling days. He's been with us just over a year and the ladies love him. I still don't know what they see in him though," Rob continued, stifling a laugh. "It must be his sparkling personality."

"It's because they like what's between my ears just as much as what's between my legs," boasted Colby, with a thick southern accent that generated an outburst of laughs from the men who were gathered nearby. "And I ain't talkin' about my cowboy boots," he said, pulling up his pant legs to reveal a pair of black snakeskin boots.

"So you're the new guy?" Colby asked Sean.

"I guess it looks that way," Sean replied, who was now standing between Derek and Raoul.

"You're gonna love it," said Colby. "It's definitely the life for me."

"What made you join the company?" asked Sean.

"I got tired of giving it away for free," Colby continued, sparking another round of claps and catcalls from the men. "I figured I needed to start charging for it." The men laughed again, as Anjelica appeared and approached Colby with a scowl on her face.

"Boys, boys, a little more discretion please," Anjelica said as the men turned towards her. "I don't want any of my clients hearing your gutter talk. It's bad for business."

"Am I in trouble, boss?" asked Colby playfully. "Would you like to spank me?"

"I would if I didn't think you'd enjoy it," Anjelica retorted, which brought another round of cheers from the men.

Just then, Sean felt a tap on his back. As he turned, he saw a younger woman standing in front of him. Smiling and wearing a black hat with her black dress, she was a brunette in her early 30s. She looked out of place at the event, as she was much younger than most of the women in the room. She stared intently at Sean as she introduced herself.

"I'm Avery," the woman said, "and you are?"

"I'm Sean," he said. "It's a pleasure to meet you."

Avery had deep, brown eyes, with large, full lips and a crooked smile. She had beautiful porcelain skin, narrow shoulders, and a stocky frame, and her voice crackled slightly with a childlike innocence.

"Are you here by yourself?" asked Avery. "If so, would you care to join me?"

"I'm sorry dear, he's spoken for," interrupted Stella, returning from the kitchen and taking Sean by the arm.

Stella led Sean into another room, closed the door, and proceeded to kiss him passionately. As he pulled Stella closer to him, he stumbled backward, pulling her with him as they fell against the wall. Sean could see that he was in a gaming room, complete with dart boards on the walls and a large, antique billiards table in its center. She pulled him closer, and they both fell backwards onto the table. They fumbled atop the surface, with Stella running her fingernails across both Sean's back and the red felt of the table. They continued to writhe and grind on each other, with Sean kissing Stella's neck and then unclasping her bra.

"Wait," she said, as Sean was unbuttoning his shirt. "Let's go upstairs."

Stella got up and took Sean's tie, leading him out of the game room and into the living room, which was not nearly as populated as before. Most of the women, as well as the Blue Shirts, were no longer there. The music continued to play loudly,

ut many of the lights had been turned off, and the darkened room had almost
ecome a large shadow unto itself. As they continued towards the staircase, they
oticed Anjelica and Avery talking near the front door. It looked as if Avery was
rying and Anjelica was trying to comfort her.

"Goodnight," Stella said to the women as she approached the stairway with
ean.

"Sweet dreams," replied Anjelica, smiling at Sean and Stella as they walked
p the staircase to the second floor.

Stella led Sean down the hallway, still holding his necktie like it was a leash.
here were several bedrooms upstairs, and as he followed Stella down the hallway,
ean noticed that most of their doors were open. While passing by, he looked into
1e first bedroom on the left, and saw one of the gigolos making love to a short,
1in woman with blonde hair. Stella glanced into the room, laughed, and closed the
oor. A few feet later, Sean looked at the open door on the right, and saw a naked
7oman, perhaps in her early 60s, blindfolded and handcuffed to the bed. Raoul
7as standing at the edge of the bed, shirtless and staring down at the woman.

"Would you like to watch?" Raoul asked. "It's okay, she doesn't mind."

Stella closed that door as well, and continued to lead Sean down the hallway.
hey bumped into a pair of women who were stumbling through the corridor, both
f whom were being followed closely by Rob and Samson. The women, who were
bviously intoxicated, mumbled a slurred "goodnight" to Sean and Stella as they
1ade their way down the hallway, bumping into the walls and each other with Rob
nd Samson close behind them.

Sean and Stella were standing at the end of the hallway, with a closed door
n either side of them. Stella reached for the door on the left when a newly familiar
oice was heard in the background.

"That room is occupied," said Colby, who was walking down the hallway
7earing only his black cowboy boots.

"I wish I could unsee that," said Sean, as he grabbed the door knob to the bedroom on the right and pulled Stella inside. Once within the dark bedroom, Stella closed the door, undressed, and pulled Sean by his tie onto the Victorian styled bed. Helped only by the light coming from the streetlights that cascaded through the blinds of the window, she undressed him. After a series of passionate kisses on his neck and chest, Stella sat on the edge of the bed and began kissing the rest of Sean's body. Standing naked in the darkness, Sean placed his hands firmly on her shoulders and watched as she pleasured him. Moments later, she fell back into the bed and stretched her arms out toward the headboard, surrendering herself to Sean. He climbed into bed beside her and began kissing her, and soon he was on top of her and inside her. Stella cried out with each thrust of Sean's hips, as her hands made their way across his shoulders down to the small of his back. After nearly an hour, they were finished, and Stella fell asleep in his arms.

As he watched her sleep, Sean pulled the covers over her and ran his hands through her hair. As she pulled closer to him, he realized that this was the first time in many years that he had sex with someone other than his wife. A few days ago he had mulled this scenario over when he agreed to join the company, and he had expected to feel conflicted about having sex with someone other than Jaclyn. Now that it was over, he felt relieved that he didn't feel burdened by guilt. Yes, as a Blue Shirt he knew that pleasing his clients sexually would be part of the job, but as he lay in this strange bed next to this strange woman, a smile came over his face. He felt happy, and after months of struggling with an unhappy marriage, he felt like he now had a purpose. Granted, much of it was far from noble, rooted in money, lust, and an underlying need to feel accepted, but part of it was different. Sean knew that he had brought joy to Stella, not just tonight but the night prior as well, and it filled him with pride and confidence. He looked at Stella and wondered what the next face that would lie beside him would look like - how she would smell, how she would feel, how she would taste.

Sean realized that he was very thirsty, so he quietly slid out of Stella's arms, left the bedroom, and began making his way downstairs toward the kitchen to get a glass of water. Wearing only his underwear, he crept down the darkened staircase. He could hear the faint sounds of music coming from the living room. Quietly he entered the room and saw Anjelica, who hadn't noticed him, swaying across the floor by herself. She was humming and singing softly along with the music, which was an old Billie Holiday song that Sean had vaguely remembered hearing earlier in the evening. She was still in her dress from the party, although she was no longer wearing her high heels. He noticed that she was holding a wine glass, which appeared to be empty, in one hand, and in her other she was holding a brown, leather bound book. It looked as if she was headed to the kitchen as well, but before she reached the doorway that led there, she stopped in front of the large oil portrait of Belle Brezing that hung on the wall nearby.

Sean watched silently as Anjelica placed her glass and book on a small bookshelf underneath the portrait. Next, she placed her hand on the right side of the portrait and pulled it slightly, which caused the frame, which was secretly hinged to the wall like a small door, to swing open. Behind the portrait was a recessed shelf that housed a combination safe, which was housed perfectly in the compartment behind the portrait. The safe, which was gray in color, had a silver dial that reflected the light emanating from the nearby lamp. Sean observed as her fingers danced across the dial, clockwise and counterclockwise, and all the while she continued to sing. Finally, she pulled the handle on the safe, opened its door, and placed the book inside.

Anjelica clumsily tried to shut the door on the safe, but Sean heard the door clank against the steel bar protruding from the handle. He then watched as she swung the portrait back towards the wall to its original position. Anjelica picked her glass up from the shelf and pivoted towards the kitchen, stumbling a bit in the process. She quickly gathered herself, giggled, and walked into the kitchen.

Sean paused for a moment, standing alone in the living room and wondering if she knew that he had been watching her. After a deep breath, he walked into the kitchen.

"You certainly believe in dressing for the occasion, don't you?" asked Anjelica flirtatiously, slurring her words slightly while looking at Sean's mostly unclothed body.

"I just wanted a glass of water," said Sean. "Stella's asleep upstairs. I didn't think that you'd mind."

"It's fine, help yourself," Anjelica replied. "I'm exhausted and going to bed. Would you be a dear and turn off the lights down here when you're done?"

"Certainly," Sean replied.

Anjelica walked towards the doorway leading to the living room, but stopped next to Sean before exiting the kitchen. She took her right hand and slid it into his underwear and squeezed his manhood.

"Don't work too hard," she said, smiling wickedly before leaving the room.

Sean shook his head and smiled, and then proceeded to find a glass in the cabinet over the sink and fill it with water from the faucet below. He tilted his head back and swallowed all of his water in one drink, and then refilled his glass. He turned off the light in the kitchen and walked back into the living room.

As he walked through the doorway, he passed the large, framed portrait on the wall, which was just a few feet to his right. He stopped and looked at the painting, which looked much more mysterious now that he knew what was concealed behind it. In the dark room, he stared at the painting, and its haunting imagery - the pensive woman in her black dress and black hat, with her dark eyes and piercing stare. He turned off the lights and walked towards the foyer to go back upstairs, but when he reached the stairway he paused. He finished his glass of water and placed it on a table next to the front door, and peered upstairs into the shadowy hallway. He knew that he needed to return to his bedroom, but he felt a greater need to return to the living room.

Moments later, he was standing directly in front of the portrait. The room was dark, with a few slivers of light coming in through the windows. With a glance over his shoulder to make sure that he was alone, Sean pulled open the frame, revealing the safe behind the portrait. Sure enough, the door of the safe was ajar from when Anjelica failed to properly close it. He slowly pulled the door open, and saw the large, brown book resting inside. He looked again towards the foyer, and then removed the book from the safe. After pushing the door of the safe back slightly, he swung the portrait back to its closed position and walked over toward the nearest window. Sean held the book up to his chest and opened it, and began to peruse its pages using the porch lights that were filtering in between the silk draperies.

As he leafed through the pages of book, he noticed that it looked to be some sort of ledger. The pages featured what appeared to be a woman's cursive handwriting, most likely Anjelica's, beautifully written in a dark blue ink upon the thick, beige paper. Atop each page was an individual woman's first and last name, as well as a series of dates and dollar amounts. Below each woman's name was a series of notes, most of which included their occupations, their phone numbers, cities of residence, and random notes about their habits and personalities. As he swiftly perused through the book, he was taken aback by some of the information he was reading, especially regarding the powerful positions that many of the women held. Some on the list were attorneys, doctors, and even elected officials. Sometimes in place of an occupation there would be a humorous phrase such as "trust fund baby", or "rich girl."

It didn't take Sean long to realize that, based on its size and the vast amount of information contained within, he was likely holding the complete financial history of all the clients who had used Blue Shirts.

After quickly flipping through most of the pages, he had arrived at the back of the book. The pages in this section featured the names of various men, as well as their contact information. He saw Rob's name, and Colby's, as well as a series of marks underneath both of their names. Turning the last page, he saw his own name, followed by some scribbled notes that were small and difficult to decipher in the shadows of the darkened room. Sean knew that this section of the book contained a list of all of the Blue Shirts that were employed by Anjelica.

Sean closed the book, placed it back in the safe, and lifted the handle on the safe as he closed its door, which locked it securely. He then closed the frame of the portrait, swinging it slowly back into place to where it was flush against the wall in its original position. As he turned away from the portrait and began walking towards the foyer, Samson appeared suddenly in the doorway.

"Can I help you?" asked Samson, with a scowl on his face.

"Shit, you scared me," said Sean, as he stopped to gather himself. "I was just down here getting some water, that's all. I'm going back upstairs though."

"Good idea," Samson replied menacingly.

Sean squeezed by Samson and continued through the narrow hallway and then up the staircase. A few moments later, he crawled back into bed with Stella, who rolled over and snuggled up to him tightly. As he closed his eyes, he found it hard to go to sleep, as he began to think of the book and the information that it contained.

Twelve

As the sun rose the next morning, so did Sean and Stella, who crept quietly into the hallway and down the staircase. The house was silent, and looked much different to Sean in the daylight. As he put Stella's coat on her and then put his on as well, he looked around and took in the calm, tranquil foyer, with its antiques and its rustic charm that seemed oddly beautiful to him. They departed the house, walking down the sidewalk and into Sean's chilly vehicle.

As the pair pulled away in the black SUV, Detective Abby Miles was watching from the driver's seat of her silver Jeep Cherokee. She pulled out a small spiral notepad, scrawled Sean's license plate number on it with a pencil, and drove away.

Once Sean and Stella arrived at the hotel room, they fell asleep almost immediately. Stella slept easily, as she was somewhat hung over from the night before, and so did Sean, who barely slept at all in Anjelica's guest bedroom. After a long rest, they spent the remainder of the afternoon visiting wineries in the southern part of the county, and later that evening they enjoyed a modest dinner at a steak house just a few blocks from the hotel.

An hour later, Sean and Stella were soaking in the garden tub in the hotel room. The hot water felt relaxing to Sean, as did the Jacuzzi jets, which was causing the bubbles in the bath to nearly overflow onto the floor.

"I can't believe that I have to leave tomorrow," Stella said, putting her wine glass on the edge of the bath. "I'm definitely not ready to go back home."

Sean thought for a moment about how much he missed his house. It had been nearly three days since he had been home, and he longed to sit on his own sofa, sleep in his own bed, but most of all, he longed to be alone. Granted, Stella's company was nice, but he was ready for some solitude.

"The weekend was amazing," Sean said as he moved closer to Stella and began slowly rubbing her shoulders. "Did you enjoy yourself?"

"Beyond words," replied Stella. "We get along so well. You're smart, funny, handsome - everything that a girl could want. I certainly hope that you find what you're looking for."

"Find what I'm looking for?" asked Sean, somewhat confused.

"You're different, Sean," Stella continued. "The other Blue Shirts are nice men, and they are always very good to me. Like you, they talk, listen, and take care of my needs in and out of the bedroom. But you have something that most of them don't have - a heart. Don't get me wrong, you're great at what you do - but I know that you have bigger and better plans for your life. I can see it in your eyes."

"You're really perceptive, I'll give that to you," Sean said with a smile.

"Well, don't worry," Stella said, "your secret is safe with me. Just promise me that you won't end up spending your next 20 years as a Blue Shirt."

"Now why would I do that?" Sean asked.

"The sex, the money, the parties - I've seen it change people," said Stella. "It can all be so addicting if you let it. It can lead you down a very dark path - so dark that you might have trouble finding your way home."

"I promise" Sean said, raising his glass and taking his last drink of wine.

The next morning, Sean and Stella walked into the airport. After a long embrace, Stella said goodbye to Sean and boarded her plane. He breathed a sigh of relief knowing that his first assignment for Blue Shirts was over. He briefly reminisced about his weekend with Stella, and felt thankful that his first client was so kind. He felt close to her, and that they shared a deeper connection beyond the companionship that he had been hired to provide to her. As he walked through the terminal, he wondered if he would ever see her again.

Sean left the airport wishing he could go home, but before he could do that he needed to pay a visit to the Chinese restaurant. It was just past 11 a.m. when he pulled into the parking lot of the Twin Dynasty, which was nestled in the corner of one of the city's newer strip malls. It was a gray, cloudy morning, but the sun was starting to peek through the clouds and reflect off of the dueling Samurai warriors that were featured in the restaurant's sign. The sweet, unmistakable aroma of Chinese food filled the parking lot as Sean walked towards the restaurant, and although he hadn't eaten since the night before, the smell didn't make him hungry.

As he nervously opened the door, Sean strode by the bubble gum machine in the lobby, and walked up to the counter. As he looked around the restaurant, there were virtually no customers at this time of day. This made it easier for him to spot the young Asian man that he had come here to find. The man was sitting alone at a table in the corner of the restaurant, talking on his cell phone and peering into the laptop computer that he had set up on his table.

A young Chinese woman came out of the kitchen and walked towards the counter to greet Sean. "Good to see you, how have you been?" she asked, beaming at Sean with a beautiful smile. The woman was Michelle, who owned the restaurant with her husband. Charming and petite, Michelle worked most everyday at the restaurant and recognized Sean immediately.

"I'm doing well, and you?" Sean replied.

"I'm good," she replied. "Just sit wherever you like and I'll be over in a minute to take your order."

"Actually, I'm here to see that guy over there," Sean said, as he nodded his head in the direction of the young Chinese man in the corner of the restaurant.

"Oh, you're here to see Ping?" Michelle said. "Okay, I'll be over in a little while to check on you."

Michelle turned away, disappearing through the silver, swinging door that led into the kitchen. Sean stood silently at the counter for a moment, wondering how he would approach the young man. He thought of Anjelica, and pessimistically imagined her reaction if Sean had to give her the news that he was unsuccessful in recruiting the Asian man into Blue Shirts. He didn't want to disappoint her, but as he stood in the restaurant and prepared to approach the young man, the reality of the situation began to take hold. He had a lot of recent experience with awkward situations, but he knew this encounter would likely rank high among them, so he drew a short breath and made his way through the restaurant, slipping past the empty chairs and tables until he was standing just a few feet away from the young man. After Sean stood there for a few seconds, the man ended the conversation on his cell phone and looked at Sean.

"Can I help you?" asked the young man in slightly broken English.

"Are you Ping?" asked Sean.

"Yeah, that's me," answered Ping.

"I'd like to speak with you if that's okay," Sean replied.

Ping nodded at Sean, and then pushed the extra chair out from under the table with his foot as a silent invitation for Sean to sit down. As Sean took his seat, he watched as Ping placed his cell phone on top of his brown wallet that was resting on the table next to the laptop. Sean noticed that there looked to be a lot of cash in the wallet, as several bills were protruding out of its side. Next to the wallet was a small plate of fried appetizers on the edge of the table, and beside it was a red plastic cup filled with soda.

Ping usually had a very unique look, and today was no exception. He was a small man, perhaps 5' 6" and 150 pounds. He was wearing a gray, pinstriped vest with a red handkerchief tucked into its front pocket, with the vest covering an ordinary white t-shirt. He was also wearing gray dress pants, also pinstriped, and a pair of white high-top sneakers, which definitely looked out of place in his ensemble. He had several rubber bands on both of his arms that he was wearing as bracelets, but Ping's most unique feature was his hair. It was shaved short on the sides, but it was long in the front and back, and although it was dark for the most part, there were streaks of blonde running throughout his hair. Ping picked up a shrimp and popped it into his mouth.

"So what do you want to talk about?" Ping asked as he swallowed the shrimp.

Sean could feel his necktie tightening as he searched for the right words. His eyes darted around the walls of the restaurant as he wondered what he might say to the stranger. He leaned in towards Ping, placing both of his elbows on the table and crossing his fingers.

"That dish looks great," Sean said nervously, as he looked at the food on Ping's plate. "What's it called?"

"Shrimp," Ping replied nonchalantly.

Sean was caught off guard by the short response he had received, and searched frantically for something else to say that could help break the ice.

"The food here is amazing," Sean continued. "All of it. The rice, the soups - everything here is great. I used to always get the General Tso's chicken but here lately I've been more of a Moo Goo Gai Pan kind of guy."

"I don't have all day," Ping said gruffly. "You gonna get to the point or what?"

Sean lowered his head and smiled, accepting of the fact that this conversation could not have been going worse. He glanced out at the parking lot through the large window at the front of the restaurant. Then he looked back at Ping.

"I know we don't really know each other," Sean said cautiously, "but my name is Sean, and I have a really unusual question to ask you."

Ping stared at Sean, took a sip from his red plastic cup filled with soda, and watched as Sean squirmed uncomfortably in his seat.

"I work for a company that is looking to hire an Asian guy for a special assignment," Sean continued.

"You think I sell drugs?" Ping asked defensively.

"No," Sean replied.

"Good, because I don't," Ping said, nibbling on one of his shrimp. "What's the special assignment?"

"How would you feel about having sex for money?" Sean asked in a hushed tone.

"With you?" replied Ping, raising his eyebrow in confusion.

"No," Sean replied, lowering his head after realizing his poor choice of words. "Let me try this again. I work for a firm that provides male companionship to wealthy women. Our company not only needs an Asian man, but we need him to start working for us tonight. And because you're literally the only Asian guy that I know - well, sort of know..."

As Sean's voiced trailed off, Ping nonchalantly picked up another shrimp and popped it into his mouth, seemingly unaffected by Sean's unusual offer. Slouching slightly in his chair, Ping wiped his mouth with his napkin and took another drink of soda. The silence was uncomfortable to Sean, who felt embarrassed about the proposal that he had just made to this young stranger.

"I'm sorry, this was a big mistake," Sean said as he rose to his feet and began to walk away. He turned away from the table and began walking through the restaurant, frustrated that the conversation with Ping went so terribly.

"Wait," Ping said, closing the screen on his laptop. "What kind of women?" he asked, with a sly smile on his face. Sean stopped, turned around, and smiled back at him.

Throughout the rest of the morning, the two men talked at the table. Sean shared with Ping most of what he knew about Blue Shirts, which sounded to Sean much like what Rob had told him at Sean's house during their first discussion about he company.

Ping's attitude continued to be subdued, but he was quietly engaged by the conversation, listening to Sean's brief history and experiences with the company. By noon, a large crowd had arrived at the restaurant for lunch, and the tables and chairs throughout the room were filled with hungry patrons. Feeling relieved that Ping appeared to be interested in the offer, as well as the conversation as a whole, Sean felt comfortable enough to order lunch. Michelle stopped by their table and Sean ordered Moo Goo Gai Pan and green tea. Ping ordered as well, speaking to Michelle in fluent Chinese. As Michelle returned to the kitchen, Ping took a long, ast drink of his soda, then proceeded to leave the table and follow Michelle back nto the kitchen. Moments later, he returned with a full cup of soda.

"You seem to have the run of the place," Sean commented.

"Michelle's my sister," Ping replied, "She lets me come and go as I please."

"So is that why I see you in here all the time?" Sean asked. "I had always assumed that you worked here."

"I used to," Ping said, brushing away with his hand a long strand of blonde hair that fell over his eye. "Michelle always wanted to own a restaurant. She got married and opened this place about seven or eight years ago. I helped her at irst - washing dishes, cooking, stuff like that. I didn't like it all that much, so on the side I started doing internet marketing. Things were slow at first, but then I started making a lot of money online. Michelle was happy for me, but my father was very skeptical about my business because he's very traditional and doesn't understand he internet. He said that I was wasting my time on the computer and that I should have a more stable career like my sister. He thinks I should be more like her, or nore like him."

"Is he in the restaurant business?" asked Sean.

"No, he's a professor at the university," Ping continued. "He's a very smart nan. He teaches math, which I was never good at - I guess that makes me the only Asian you will ever meet that sucks at math."

Both men laughed as Michelle returned to their table with their entrees. Sean was surprised to see the large amount of food that she had placed in front of her diminutive brother. Ping immediately opened a set of chopsticks and began stirring a large bowl of noodles that was directly in front of him.

"My father should be proud of us," continued Ping, as the steam rose from his bowl. "He and my mother raised two successful children. Michelle and her husband expanded and now own 2 other restaurants in the city, so they are doing very well for themselves. He is proud of her, but he isn't proud of me because he doesn't understand what I do."

"So why are you in here all the time?" Sean asked.

"Because I'm bored," shared Ping. "I work some from home but after a while that gets old. I can work just about anywhere as long as I have a good wi-fi signal. I like to come here and see my sister, and I like the food."

Both men laughed again and started eating their lunches.

"Maybe it's not that you're bored," commented Sean. "Maybe you come in here because you're lonely. It sounds like you don't get to meet a lot of people in your line of work, especially if you're chained to a computer all day."

"If I accept your proposal, what would the next step be?" Ping asked, as he twirled the noodles in his bowl with his chopsticks

The two men shared a smile, and Sean was quietly elated that it looked like Ping was on the cusp of agreeing to join Blue Shirts. More so, Sean felt a kinship with the young man, and it seemed clear to him that this new friendship was reciprocated.

"After lunch," Sean said, "I will introduce you to Anjelica. She will go over all of the particulars with you, from what you'll be wearing to what you'll be driving and everything in between. Your first client arrives tonight, and will likely be in town for the next 3 days. This means that you'll be with her 24/7 until Thursday. If everything goes well, Anjelica will provide you with more clients."

As Ping wiped his mouth with his napkin, Sean watched as his new friend contemplated the offer. In this silence, Sean considered his own reasons for being a Blue Shirt, and wondered if bringing Ping into this lifestyle was a good idea. Even though he knew the answer to that question, he rationalized that his own livelihood depended on Blue Shirts, and that fulfilling Anjelica's request of recruiting Ping was necessary for his own survival at the company.

"She's going to have a few questions for you," Sean added. "For instance, she'll want to know how much experience that you've had with women - how many you've been with, and other questions like that."

"I've had many girlfriends," Ping responded, "but not many lately. In my line of work it's hard to maintain a relationship. Girls all the time want to text all day and talk all night. I don't have time for that. But I know how to take care of a woman when I need to - what they want, what they like - so she doesn't need to worry about that."

"That's good to hear," replied Sean.

"What do these women look like?" Ping asked, as he leaned slightly backward in his chair. "You said that they are older, but are any of them pretty?"

"Most of the ones that I have met so far are beautiful," Sean replied. "They tend to take really good care of themselves. I would guess that because they are wealthy, they spend a lot of time and money to make them beautiful on the outside. But if you believe that true beauty comes from within, then I doubt that you'll be disappointed with the women you will meet."

"You bullshit just like a white guy," Ping said, laughing as he ran his fingers through his hair, scratching his scalp in the process.

"So what do you say?" Sean asked, tilting his head and laughing along with Ping.

"There is an old Chinese proverb," Ping said, as his eyes slowly shifted towards the colorful mural on the restaurant's wall. "There are four things that won't come back: the spoken word, the spent arrow, the past life, and the neglected opportunity."

"Those are very wise words," added Sean.

"It sounds fun," said Ping, whose smile grew larger. "Count me in."

Thirteen

Sean couldn't remember being this tired as he pulled into his driveway and slowly guided his truck into the garage. He removed his overnight bag from his truck and walked into his dark basement, then proceeded to lumber up the stairway into the stark brightness of his living room. He grabbed a bottle of water from his refrigerator, taking a drink as he leaned across the backrest of one of the stools by the kitchen counter. It was early in the afternoon, but it had already been an exhausting day. He walked into his bedroom, adjusted the blinds on his window, and looked longingly at his large, king-sized bed. It had never looked so inviting, and he knew that a long nap was in his very near future. While drawing the curtains, he decided to make a quick phone call to Anjelica to share the good news about his meeting with Ping.

"The guy from the restaurant is good to go," he said, after Anjelica answered the phone. "I gave him your number, so he should be calling you soon."

"I just got off the phone with him," exclaimed Anjelica. "He's on his way over now. Thank you so much, Sean - you really came through for me and I certainly appreciate it."

"I'm happy to help," Sean said, removing his shirt while holding his phone.

"Did you and Stella enjoy yourselves on Saturday night?" asked Anjelica. "What did you think of the party?"

"It was interesting," Sean said, "and she had a great time. It was a good weekend all around - I'm sure that she was pleased."

"That's so good to hear," Anjelica replied. "I know that you're probably tired, so I'll let you go - oh, I almost forgot - are you available this weekend? It's not definite yet, but it's looking like your services are being personally requested."

"Yes, I'm pretty sure I can make that happen," replied Sean.

"Excellent, I'll be in touch," said Anjelica.

After the conversation, Sean dropped his phone onto the soft, white bed sheets and sat on the edge of his bed, removing his shoes and socks. He then fell backwards into his bed, staring at the white ceiling above him. A slight breeze wafted through the room, coming from the slow-turning blades of the ceiling fan circling above him. He closed his eyes and had almost drifted off to sleep when his cell phone beeped. He frowned, opened his eyes and slowly retrieved his phone, which was lying beside him.

As he looked at his phone, Sean was pleasantly surprised to see that the beep was an email notification alerting him that he had just received a deposit into his Paypal account. He opened the email, and to his surprise $7,500 had been deposited into his account. As he examined the email further, he saw a scanned copy of Stella's receipt for Blue Shirts, containing a basic breakdown of his compensation for his weekend with Stella. His $5,000 payment from the company for "services rendered" was listed on the receipt, as was a $2,500 gratuity from Stella.

Because the last few days had been such a blur, Sean had nearly forgotten that he was being paid for what he was doing. "Services rendered," he mumbled to himself, chuckling slightly at the phrase's hidden meanings, as he fell back into his bed and watched the ceiling fan continue to turn.

By nightfall, Sean was wide awake and was feeling productive. In a white t-shirt and blue flannel pajama pants, he gathered up his clothes from his hamper and started a load of laundry. He loaded the dishwasher, and watered the plants that were scattered throughout the house, most of which were browning slightly due to neglect. He was happy to be home again, and the household chores that were almost always a nuisance to him were now fun in an odd sort of way. The financial benefits of his new job had alleviated much of the stress that he had endured over the last week, and the appreciation that Stella, as well as Anjelica, had given him had restored his self confidence. It had been several months since he had been this happy, and he was cautiously excited to see what future journeys were in store for him.

He felt rested and recharged, so much so that when Rob texted to tell Sean that he was coming by and bringing pizza, he didn't refuse.

An hour later, the doorbell rang and Sean answered the door. It was Rob, holding a large pizza box, as well as Colby, the Blue Shirt who Sean had met at Anjelica's party.

"Hey there fellah," Colby said, brandishing a case of beer as he walked into Sean's living room.

"You remember Colby," Rob said as he placed the pizza on the kitchen counter. "We were in the neighborhood and thought that you might be hungry."

"And thirsty," added Colby, as he pulled three bottles of beer from the case and placed the rest of the beer in the refrigerator.

"I'm happy to see that you're wearing more than boots this time," Sean said, prompting a big round of laughs from the men.

"You and me both," Colby replied as he popped the cap off of his beer bottle and took a drink. "But buck naked in boots I still dress better than that Chinaman that's working with us now. Where'd you find him anyway? Did he recently get kicked out of a boy band?"

"So I take it you guys met him?" Sean inquired.

"We were at Anjelica's house when he came by," Rob answered as he devoured the pizza. "His hair is a little over the top, but she thinks that the client is going to like him."

"What did you think of him?" asked Sean.

"He was very professional," Rob continued. "He showed up in a blue dress shirt, black pants - I've got to hand it to him, he was well-prepared and looked the part. Anjelica spent about an hour preparing him, and when he was good and ready she sent him off to the airport to pick up his date."

"In my Escalade," Colby added while swallowing a bite of pizza.

"What?" Sean asked.

"He didn't have an SUV so Anjelica asked me to let him borrow my damn Escalade," said Colby, as he smiled and took a drink of beer. "Believe me, if he crashes it up I'm gonna tear him a new one."

"Well, he's the best I could do on short notice," Sean said, shrugging his shoulders and taking another drink of beer.

"Well, next time get somebody taller," Colby continued. "He barely comes up to my damn waist. When he's standing beside me we look like Mr. Roarke and Tattoo. I kept waiting for him to yell out 'da plane', 'da plane'!"

"Colby's just giving you shit, Sean, don't worry about it," said Rob, while opening his beer and taking a slice of pizza from the box. "Ping is going to work out just fine."

"Anyway," Rob added, "he's going to check in with Anjelica later tonight to let her know how his date is going. She said that she'd call me as soon as she hears from him to give me an update. By the way, did you get paid yet for this past weekend?"

"I did," Sean said. "It really came in handy too."

"How much did you get tipped?" Colby asked.

"$2,500," Sean responded with sly grin.

"Son of a bitch!" Colby shouted with a smile on his face. "I've never gotten a tip that big."

"I guess I just got lucky," Sean replied as he took a bite of pizza.

"Gettin' lucky for gettin' lucky," Colby responded, while taking a large gulp from his beer. "God, I love America."

"Colby might be a little rough around the edges," shared Rob, "but he's one of Anjelica's favorites. And although we all must follow a certain set of guidelines, she prides herself on having an eclectic mix of employees to accommodate the varying tastes of her clients. We're all unique in our way and bring different personalities to the table. If a client is into black guys, there's Samson. If they want a Latin lover, there's Raoul."

"If they want a redneck, they get me," Colby said with a deadpan expression, which soon turned into an outburst of laughter.

"If they want a southern gentleman, they get Colby" Rob added, with an equally serious expression, "We all have our roles."

"Really?" asked Sean as he smiled and took a drink of his beer. "Then what's my role?"

"Right now, it's getting me another beer," Rob responded with a cocky grin.

Sean smiled, opened his refrigerator, and handed Rob another bottle of beer. Colby took a seat on the barstool and pulled another piece of pizza from the box on the counter. As he pulled his cell phone out of the pocket of his blue jeans, Colby glanced at it, rolled his eyes and started texting with a slightly downtrodden look on his face.

"Sorry boys, it's the fiancée," Colby muttered.

"Fiancée?" asked Sean.

"Yeah, she wants to know if I'm coming home tonight," Colby responded to Sean as he continued to type on his phone.

"His situation isn't all that unique," Rob explained to Sean. "Some of the

Blue Shirts have serious girlfriends, but most of us don't because it's so difficult to keep what we do a secret from them. Derek, whom you met at the party, is actually married - his wife lives in Vegas and she thinks that he's a pilot for one of the airlines, which helps him explain all of the travel that he has to do."

"So how do you explain all of the strange hours to your fiancée?" Sean asked Colby. "Do you tell her that you're spending all those weekends planning the wedding?"

"Well I sure as hell don't tell her that I'm out bangin' broads for a living, that's for damn sure," Colby replied, while setting his cell phone on the counter and taking a quick drink of beer. "She thinks that I'm a fireman."

"A fireman?" Sean responded.

"Yep," Colby replied. "I told her when we met that I work in a department in Covington and that I'd be working a lot of weekends."

"Covington?" Sean asked. "That's 90 miles away."

"Yep," Colby continued as the men smiled. "I told her that the pay was way better up there and that's why I didn't want to work here in Lexington."

"What if she calls the station to check up on you?" Sean asked. "Won't she find out that you don't work there?"

"I gave her Rob's number," Colby replied. "That way when she calls, he sees that it's her and he answers it 'Covington Fire Department'. He then always tells her that I'm out on a run or doing something at that moment, but that he'll radio me and have me call her back as soon as I can."

"Wow," Sean replied. "So where did you come up with that story? Did you use to be a fireman?"

"Hell no," said Colby, stifling a laugh. "But it was either that or tell her that I'm a spy. I figured this would be more believable."

"Good point," replied Sean, shaking his head and smiling.

"Gentlemen," Rob interjected, as he slowly lifted his bottle into the air, "I would like to propose a toast. To new friends, and new possibilities."

Sean and Colby smiled, raised their bottles, and clanked them against Rob's.

Fourteen

The next day, Sean skipped his usual morning shower, and left his house early to run errands. In blue jeans, sneakers, t-shirt and a flannel pullover, he felt relieved to be wearing something other than the dress clothes that he had been confined to for most of the last few days. The red baseball cap he was wearing felt good on his head, and he loosened it slightly to help alleviate the slight headache that he had from drinking with Rob and Colby the night before.

Sean parked and exited his truck, then slung a weekend's worth of blue dress shirts over his shoulder and walked into the dry cleaners. A young lady was working behind the counter helping another customer, so as Sean waited for her to finish, he glanced at his cell phone and scrolled through the unread texts that he had recently received.

"Everything is going well," reported Ping, who evidently had texted him very early in the morning.

"Call me," messaged Jaclyn, which prompted a sigh from Sean, as he suspected that her short text meant that she was upset at him for something he had done.

Suddenly, a loud alert sounded from the phone, the same familiar tone that Sean remembered from the park last week. Distracted and embarrassed by the loud noise emanating from his phone, he looked up to see that he was next in line. He hurriedly handed the young employee his shirts and began to walk away.

"Excuse me, I'm sorry" Sean said to the young lady, as he laid his shirts on the counter and walked outside onto the sidewalk. Looking at his phone he realized that the alert was from Blue Shirts, and that another job was in his near future.

Across town, Detective Tom Wyatt was at the Lexington Police Department, sitting at his desk and talking on the phone. He was leaning back in his creaky chair, twirling a pencil in his right hand when Detective Abby Miles came up beside him and sat on the edge of his desk. Wyatt abruptly ended his conversation, and laid his pencil down on his desk.

"I did a little checking up on that guy you met at the airport," Abby said.

"A little checking up?" Wyatt inquired, with a wry smile on his face, taking one of the cups of coffee from Abby.

"Okay, a lot of checking up," Abby said, taking a sip of her coffee.

"What exactly did you do?" asked Wyatt.

"I had a PI friend of mine run a fairly thorough check on your guy, and he came up clean," Abby replied, as she pulled her spiral notebook out of her jacket pocket and began reading off the information contained within. "Sean Everett has no criminal history, worked as a stockbroker at Kenley & Logan for a while but got laid off. He's recently divorced - he got the house in the country, she bought a condo in the city - and they share custody of an adolescent son."

"At the airport he told me that he was a chauffer," Wyatt said, while furrowing his brow. "I guess he went from closing deals to providing wheels."

"I tailed him the other night," Abby said, as Wyatt, looking surprised, began shifting in his seat in disapproval. "I know, you're probably going to say that I shouldn't have, but I did. Anyway, he spent the night at a house off Short Street owned by Anjelica Reardon. Ever hear of her?"

"I can't say that I have," replied Wyatt.

"Me neither," Abby continued. "Her house is definitely in the high rent district, so she's probably got some money. I'll poke around and see what I can find out about her."

"Sounds good," Wyatt said, taking another sip of coffee. "Did you see anything unusual?"

"Only that apparently you have to have a black SUV to get invited to her parties," Abby responded. "Nothing but fleet vehicles lined up and down the street, all black. It looked like a damn Secret Service convention."

"Interesting," Wyatt said.

Another veteran officer, Sergeant Ray Blackburn, approached Wyatt and Abby and dropped a small stack of papers on Wyatt's desk.

"It's probably nothing," Abby continued. "I doubt that he's involved in anything too shady considering that his father is none other than Jack Everett."

"The Jack Everett?" responded Wyatt, with a pained grimace on his face. "No legacy is so rich as honesty."

"Let me guess," Abby said, tilting her head sideways. "Hamlet? King Lear?"

"All's Well That Ends Well, actually," replied Wyatt, who appeared to be growing angry and agitated as his voice became deeper and more aggressive. "One of Shakespeare's finest works, but nice try, my dear."

Wyatt rose quickly from his chair, passing between Abby and Sergeant Blackburn on his way out of the office.

"Tom, are you okay?" Abby asked, as Wyatt stormed out of the room. Abby then turned to look at Sergeant Blackburn. "What was that all about?"

"You don't know?" Blackburn asked her.

"That Jack Everett is a legend, a hero?" Abby responded. "I've heard the stories."

"Tom's dad was 'Buckeye' Wyatt," added Blackburn, "the DA that tried to get Everett to testify in the Spradlin trial. The city had a lot invested in that case, but not nearly as much as Tom's dad. He was a pretty big deal at the time, and word on the street was that he was eyeing a run for Senator after the trial. The case was big news around here, especially after 'Buckeye' guaranteed that he was going to get a conviction."

"How strong was their case against Spradlin?" Abby asked.

"Good, but not great," Blackburn responded. "With Everett's testimony, it was a slam dunk. He was Spradlin's partner so he saw a lot and knew a lot. Without Everett, it could have gone either way. When the jury came back in with a not guilty verdict, Tom's dad was devastated and humiliated. The public blamed 'Buckeye' for failing to win the trial, so they voted him out of office in the next election, sending his political aspirations down the tubes. He never got over it. Soon he was out of work, and he had trouble finding another job because of the public failure he had endured. He started hitting the bottle pretty hard, and eventually drank himself to death."

"I had no idea," Abby said. "He's never talked about that with me."

"It's a sore subject, that's for sure," shared Blackburn. "Sure, Jack Everett may be a hero to a lot of us here at the department, but to Tom? He's the man who killed his father."

Fifteen

As he quickly made his way out of the police station and into the afternoon sunlight, Detective Wyatt was approached on the front steps of the building by a heavy-set man in a suit.

"Now's not a good time, Floss," grumbled Wyatt, as he continued walking past the man and down the stairs onto the sidewalk.

"It's great to see you too, Tom," said the man sarcastically as he started following Wyatt's footsteps.

The man was Arnie Floss, one of Lexington's most notorious defense attorneys. Dressed in a dark gray, pinstriped business suit and a large, yellow necktie, Floss was one of the city's most flamboyant lawyers. A large man in his early 50s, Floss had a receding hairline of jet black hair, peppered with just a bit of gray on the sides. He had known Wyatt for a few years, as he had represented in court many of the men whom Wyatt had arrested and brought to justice. Floss was an excellent trial lawyer, but was better known as a slick talker who was very capable of securing plea deals for his clients before their trials would begin. Despite his open dislike of Floss, occasionally working with him had become a necessary evil for Wyatt, who sometimes found it best to negotiate a deal with the brash and abrasive attorney in order to ensure a conviction in court.

"I have someone that wants to talk to you," Floss said, breathing heavily from trying to keep pace with Wyatt. "It's Dr. Luzzato."

"Whatever he has to say, he can say back there," said Wyatt, and he pointed over his shoulder at the police station as he continued to walk briskly down the sidewalk.

"No, he can't," replied Floss, as he continued to follow Wyatt. "Besides, you'll want to hear this."

"Let me guess," Wyatt responded, stopping and turning to face Floss. "He wants a deal? No dice. His case is airtight and he's going to be going away for a long time."

"That may very well be, Tom, but he has something important that he wants to speak with you about first," Floss replied, glistening in perspiration from his lumbering pursuit.

"All right, fine," Wyatt said, "I've got some time now if you want to bring him back to the station."

"Now is good," Floss replied, "however Dr. Luzzato would like to meet in a more discreet location. He doesn't particularly care for your interrogation room - he found his last experience there to be rather unpleasant."

"Where then?" asked Wyatt impatiently.

"The address is inside here," Floss responded as he handed Wyatt a plain, white envelope. "See you in an hour, and come alone."

Wyatt took the envelope and watched as Floss smiled, turned and walked back down the sidewalk. A half hour later, Wyatt was inside his car. As he sat behind the steering wheel, he drew a deep breath, and leaned his head back against the seat's headrest. He opened the envelope, and read the note within it. The address on the note was for an abandoned factory building on Manchester Street, in an area just a couple miles west of downtown. As he made the short drive through the city, Wyatt arrived at the building. He pulled into the parking lot, which was overrun with grass and weeds that had been seeping through the cracks in the concrete over the years. Next to the building was a new black Lexus, shimmering in the sunlight, and looked rather out of place in this distressed environment.

As Wyatt exited his car, he looked up at the rustic, 6-story building, with its crumbling red brick and its broken windows. Time had not been kind to the structure, which had once been an active, thriving factory several decades before. The steel front doors of the edifice, which were covered in chipped beige paint, were wide open. Wyatt unbuttoned his trench coat, and removed the Glock 22 handgun that had been securely hidden in his shoulder holster.

Stepping carefully through the building, Wyatt ascended the ghostly staircase. The walls were drab and gray, and the wooden railings were hanging loosely off the walls of the stairwell. As he arrived at the top floor of the building, he walked into a desolate hallway. Doors lined both sides of the corridor, all of which were closed shut, but at the end of corridor was a door that was wide open. As he tread over the yellowing newspapers and other assorted garbage that was scattered across the floor, Wyatt, with his gun still drawn, stepped quietly through the hallway until he arrived at a door that was slightly cracked open. As he pushed the door, a loud creak filled the air, and he tightened the grip on his gun. As he looked into the vast expanse of the room that lie ahead, he could see that its walls were covered in spray-painted graffiti, and he could make out a few exposed pipes that were dangling from the ceiling. A light layer of dust floated about, visible in the thin rays of sunlight that spilled into the room through the broken windows. Toward the end of the room he saw two men sitting beside an old, dented steel table.

"Come in, Tom," said Floss, his voice echoing throughout the spacious room. "And put that away - I don't feel like getting shot today."

As he approached the men, Detective Wyatt saw Floss rise from his chair. Beside him was Dr. Paul Luzzato, who remained seated with a nervous look on his face as Wyatt arrived at the table. A dermatologist who had built a small but successful practice over the years, Luzzato was a short, thin man in his late 50s, with graying brown hair parted to the side. He was wearing thin, wire frame glasses that he was frequently pushing up the bridge of his nose with his finger. Wearing khaki pants, a brown leather jacket, and white tennis shoes, he fidgeted in his chair as Wyatt glared at him. Luzzato had recently been arrested by Wyatt for writing bogus prescriptions for a variety of prescription drugs, including OxyContin, Vicadin, Xanax and Valium. During a sting operation that culminated with his arrest during a raid of his office, Wyatt and his fellow officers found a stockpile of controlled substances and almost $60,000 in cash hidden away in his office. It had also become obvious to the officers during their investigation that Luzzato was an addict himself, indicated by his erratic behavior and by the large amount of medication that was also found at his home, including several prescriptions that he had forged using fake names and various medical aliases. Even though he was facing substantial charges, Dr. Luzzato posted bond shortly thereafter and was awaiting trial.

Floss pulled out a black security wand and slowly approached Wyatt.

"Is this really necessary?" Wyatt asked.

"We just want to make sure that you're not wired," Floss replied, as he waved the wand across Wyatt's body.

Wyatt opened his trench coat as Floss waved the wand across the holster, which elicited a loud chirp from the device. He continued to scan Wyatt from head to toe, satisfied that the detective had not brought any surveillance equipment to the meeting.

"Have a seat," Floss said to Detective Wyatt, who reluctantly pulled out a metal folding chair from under the table and sat down facing the men.

"Dr. Luzzato is sorry about all of the trouble that he's caused," Floss said. "He understands that he has brought a great deal of hardship to those involved in this matter, and he would like to put this unpleasantness behind him. You see, the people who he supplied with medication are sick. They are addicts who have almost no control over their behavior. Dr. Luzzato understands what their situations are and sympathizes with these people, because he too has struggled with addiction himself. That being said, he is willing to provide testimony against his former patients in exchange for full immunity from prosecution on all of the charges that you have against him. He talks, he walks - it's that simple."

"He's a true humanitarian, huh?" Wyatt responded sarcastically. "He also cares about his own patients so much so that he's willing to throw them all under the bus just to save his own ass. Well, the truth is that Luzzato's the closest thing that the city's had to a drug kingpin in a long time, and we have enough evidence to put him away for quite a while. Same goes for all of the 'sick' people that he was writing fake scrips for over the last few years."

"The cases against his patients are strong, but they aren't iron clad," replied Floss. "With his testimony, most of them won't even go to trial. You'd have the convictions you want, and you'd be saving the taxpayers a lot of money."

"I'm not interested," Wyatt replied. "And why you brought me down here to talk about this is beyond me. We could have easily discussed this at the station."

Wyatt stood up and began to leave, as Dr. Luzzato desperately looked at Floss.

"Just a minute," Floss said with urgency in his voice. "Before you leave, the good doctor has a story to tell you. Now bear in mind this is all off the record. It's just a story - nothing more, nothing less."

Wyatt looked at Floss but then turned towards Dr. Luzzato, who nervously glanced at both Floss and Wyatt as he trembled in his chair. Luzzato's eyes darted around the room before finally fixating on Wyatt.

"Have you ever heard of a 'Botox party', Detective?" asked Dr. Luzzato, leaning forward and placing his gloved hands on the dusty table.

"I can't say that I have," Wyatt dryly responded as he slowly sat back down.

"Not long ago, a patient of mine invited me to her home for a dinner party," continued Luzzato, tracing a circle with his finger on the dusty surface of the table. "After accepting her invitation, she informed me that most of her guests would be women, many of whom loved Botox. She asked me to bring some with me that night, and I happily obliged. After some drinks, my hostess placed me at a table in the corner of her living room. One by one, the women at the party came forward and I gave them Botox injections. It was quite surreal actually."

"Sounds like a waste of time," Wyatt commented. "Kind of like this conversation that we're having."

"I was such a big hit that she invited me back, again and again," said Luzzato, whose pale skin began to perspire. "Before long I had gained her trust, not only as her doctor but also as her friend. As the parties continued, I looked around, listened, and watched what was going on within the walls of that house. It didn't take long to realize that she was running a high-end prostitution service."

"So the women you were injecting were call girls?" asked Wyatt.

"No," the doctor interjected, "they were clients. It's the men at these parties that are the prostitutes. Anjelica hires them and turns them into gigolos."

"Anjelica?" Wyatt asked. "Who's Anjelica?"

"Anjelica Reardon," responded Luzzato. "She's the 'madam', or whatever they're calling it these days."

Detective Wyatt instantly recognized Anjelica's name from his earlier conversation at the police station with Abby. He knew that Luzzato was unstable, and his nervous twitching suggested that he was currently under the influence of one of the controlled substances he had been arrested for prescribing. Luzzato had a shady reputation, and he also knew that the doctor was facing a long prison sentence once his trial began. Wyatt knew that most, if not all, of his story could have been invented in order to give him a bargaining chip in a plea deal. But no matter how hard he tried, Wyatt couldn't hold his bad memories of Jack Everett at bay. He thought about the encounter with Jack's son, Sean Everett, at the airport. Then he wondered who exactly was Anjelica Reardon, and was it possible that this mysterious woman could be running a male prostitution ring in Lexington? Wyatt also wondered why Abby saw Sean Everett at Anjelica Reardon's house this past weekend. Did Sean Everett simply know this woman, or was there a working relationship between the two? Finally, could it be that this desperate, pill-addicted doctor was telling the truth?

"The doc knows a lot more," Floss said, "but that's all you get for now. You'll get much more if you're willing to work with us."

"That's all very well and good," Wyatt commented, "but prostitution is just about on par with jaywalking. It's barely even on the department's radar anymore."

"This is more than just common street level prostitution," replied Floss, "The women involved are loaded, and they're paying big money to hook up with these pretty boys."

"We're still talking about a slap on the wrist," responded Wyatt. "Maybe some time for Ms. Reardon but nothing substantial."

"Not with the kind of money that these ladies are throwing around," Floss continued. "You get the IRS involved and it'll create a shit storm. Lots of prison time for everyone involved."

"That's how they got Capone," interjected Luzzato, with his voice trailing off as he smiled meekly at Wyatt.

"The public would eat this up," Floss said, after rolling his eyes at Luzzato. "It would be the lead-in on every TV station and the front page in all the newspapers. As the lead investigator you'd be the big hero. Everybody would know your name."

"I'm not looking for publicity," Wyatt countered.

"Then do it because it's the right thing to do," Floss responded passionately. "You have a reputation at the department as a boy scout and a bulldog rolled into one. You hate crime, and you hate criminals even more. I know you, Tom, and I know that you're not going to ignore what we've told you today. Sure, right now you might think what Anjelica Reardon is doing is small potatoes, but it's going to eat at you, and sooner or later you'll be wanting to bring her operation down. You know why? Because it's big, and because it's criminal, and because it's happening in your city!"

Detective Wyatt stood up again, turned, and began walking hastily towards the doorway.

"You're going to need us, Tom!" exclaimed Floss, as Wyatt disappeared through the doorway. "If you want to bring her down, you're going to need us!"

Sixteen

It was Tuesday night, and Sean was in his living room enjoying a quiet evening with Braden. They were watching a University of Kentucky basketball game on television, cheering on their beloved Wildcats to a come-from-behind victory in the closing seconds of the game. Braden, in a white t-shirt and blue flannel pajama pants, was seated with his legs crossed on the smaller couch. Sean, who was sitting on the larger couch in a similar outfit, was finishing a plate of buffalo wings that he and Braden were sharing. As Braden left the room to begin getting ready for bed, Sean took their plates into the kitchen and placed them in the sink.

After running water over the plates and drying his hands with the dish towel, Sean picked up his phone to look again at his latest assignment for the company. After getting the alert this morning at the dry cleaners, he had glanced at the assignment off and on throughout the rest of the day. His new client's last name was 'Kincaid', but there was no flight arrival information, only the phrase "This Friday", followed by "Call for Details." Sean was happy to be working again so soon, and assumed that the client hadn't finalized her flight details yet, so he decided that he would call Anjelica tomorrow morning for further pickup instructions. Meanwhile, he found himself being intrigued about the client. He wondered what she would look like, what her background would be, and if she would be as warm and friendly as Stella.

From the kitchen, Sean saw the bright movement of a car's headlights spilling through the front windows of his house. As he walked to the front door, he could see that the vehicle was Jaclyn's. After parking and exiting her car, she walked up the concrete steps carrying a white cloth shoulder bag. With the front door open, Sean watched silently as Jaclyn approached him.

"Didn't you get my text?" asked Jaclyn angrily, as she walked past Sean and into the house.

"I did, it's just that I didn't have time to call you today," Sean replied.

"Mom!" exclaimed Braden, who rushed over to hug his mother as he dangled a toothbrush from his mouth. "What are you doing here?"

"Hi, honey," Jaclyn said to Braden. "I just wanted to come over and visit with you and your dad tonight, that's all."

After embracing his mother, Braden returned to his bathroom to finish brushing his teeth. Jaclyn walked into the kitchen, removed her hat and gloves and placed them on the counter.

"Is everything okay," Sean asked with a concerned look on his face.

"I need to ask you something," said Jaclyn, as she placed her bag on the kitchen counter and removed her coat, draping it over the backrest of one of the barstools.

"Okay, shoot." Sean responded.

"This may sound a little crazy, but I think someone is following me," Jaclyn replied. "Yesterday, when I was at my office, I saw a lady in the parking lot sitting in her car. She was there most of the afternoon. I thought that she might be someone's client, so I asked everyone in the office if they knew her and they said 'no'. After a while we sent Will Conley out there to ask her why she was there, and when she saw him coming she drove off."

"If I saw Will Conley coming at me I'd probably drive off too," Sean joked.

"I'm being serious, Sean," Jaclyn said with a smirk. "This morning, I was showing property and I saw her again, this time in my rearview mirror. Same woman, same car."

"What kind of car?" Sean replied.

"A silver Jeep," Jaclyn responded. "I think it was a Cherokee."

"I see," Sean said, pausing for a moment. "You don't think that I have something to do with that, do you?"

"All I know is that since I moved out, things have been really weird," Jaclyn replied. "Are you mixed up in anything that I should know about?"

"No, of course not," said Sean, "what would give you that idea?"

"I'm scared Sean," Jaclyn said. "What if she knows where I live? I'm not going home knowing that she could be waiting for me my house right now. I'm staying here tonight."

"Okay, that's fine," Sean replied, "you can sleep on the couch."

"The couch?" responded Jaclyn, as she folded her arms.

"Do you have a problem with that?" asked Sean.

"That's fine," Jaclyn replied. "I just thought that you'd offer me a bed, considering all that I've been through tonight."

"Well, this is my house now, which means that the bed in the master bedroom is mine," Sean said with a smirk. "I'd be happy to let you stay in one of the guest rooms but they don't have any beds in them. You took them with you when you left me, remember?"

After Braden went to bed, Sean pulled a pillow and blanket from the shelf of the hall closet and placed them on the armrest of the couch, then disappeared into his bedroom and closed the door. Jaclyn remained in the living room, standing by the couch and fluffing the old, worn-out pillow that was crumpled up in front of her. She laid down and covered herself with the musty blanket. She found it difficult to find a comfortable position on the sofa, and even more difficult to fall asleep, as she was still preoccupied by the night's events. The living room was dark, although the porch lights from the front and back of the house provided enough light to see most everything around her.

Sean wasn't that tired either, but it was almost midnight, and he knew that he would be taking Braden to school early the next morning. As he lay alone in his large bed, he replayed the conversation that he had with Jaclyn earlier in the evening, and wondered if someone might actually be following her. He knew that if what she said was true, there was a good chance that it might be connected to his new line of work. He wondered if the woman who followed Jaclyn tonight was a client, or perhaps even Anjelica herself.

Moments after falling asleep, Sean heard his bedroom door open. He watched as Jaclyn walked through the doorway and approached his bed, eventually standing over him.

"I'm too scared to sleep by myself," she whispered to him, hovering over him in a pink tank top and white shorts.

Without a word, Sean watched as Jaclyn climbed into his bed. He removed his t-shirt, and walked to the other side of the bed, pulling the covers back. Seconds later, Jaclyn slid closer to him, nuzzling her head on his shoulder as she placed her arm over his chest. Surprised, Sean titled his head towards her until their eyes met. Jaclyn kissed Sean, briefly at first, as she pulled herself closer to him until she was straddling him. As she continued to stare at him, Sean could sense that she considered him to be her protector, and that she felt safe with him. He also sensed a deeper need in her, and saw in her eyes a reawakened passion that had been missing for many months. Sean began kissing her neck, groping and fondling her as she passionately returned his caresses. As they began to make love, Jaclyn placed her arms around Sean's neck, pulling herself even closer to him. For the next hour, their bodies moved in perfect rhythm. Breathless and sweaty, they both collapsed backwards, falling next to each other in the center of the bed.

"Well, that was unexpected," Sean said, as he peered through the darkness at Jaclyn.

"Do you remember the last time that we made love?" Jaclyn asked.

"Not off hand," Sean replied curiously.

"It was Labor Day weekend," Jaclyn continued. "That's almost 6 months ago."

"The resort, right?" asked Sean. "I remember. My folks watched the kids so we could get away for the weekend. It was nice."

"Are you seeing someone?" Jaclyn asked, slowly pulling the bed sheet up in an effort to cover her naked body.

"What?" Sean responded, as he turned to face her.

"Braden said that you brought a woman to his school with you last week," Jaclyn replied, "and that she went with you to his orthodontist appointment."

"She's just a client," Sean said defiantly. "I was hired to drive her around, that's all. It's nothing. And did he tell you that she's old enough to be my mother?"

"Well, it just sounds strange," Jaclyn responded. "I haven't been with anyone since the last time I was with you. No sex, not even a single date. I know that guys are different than women after a divorce, and I sincerely doubt that you could go that many months without sex. I thought for sure that you would at least be dating someone by now."

"Well, I haven't," Sean replied, pausing for a few seconds as he continued to look at Jaclyn. "Not even a single date?"

"Will Conley asked me out, but I turned him down," Jaclyn responded.

"I knew he always liked you," Sean replied as he shook his head and smiled. "Why did you turn him down?"

"Because he's a creep," Jaclyn replied, as she and Sean began laughing loudly. She turned to face Sean, snuggling up to him again as she pulled the comforter over their bodies.

The next morning, Sean crept into the kitchen and made a pot of coffee. Jaclyn began to stir, but she decided to remain in the warm bed for the time being. Braden emerged from his bedroom, dressed in blue jeans, high top sneakers, and a long sleeve t-shirt. Braden grabbed a Pop-Tart from the pantry and followed his father into the garage. As they left their house, Sean took a sip of coffee from his thermos, and quietly contemplated his night with Jaclyn as he drove to Braden's school. He wondered if the previous night's events meant that they were now back together, or if at least Jaclyn would believe that they were. He knew that she wasn't a very impulsive person, and that the choices she made, including last night's decision to sleep with him, were usually well thought out. She was also a woman who trusted her heart even more than her instincts, and was now at the very least considering a reconciliation.

After hugging Braden and dropping him off at school, Sean began to question the situation even further. He was surprised to find that he was conflicted about his emotions with Jaclyn. Part of him still loved her, and he could easily imagine picking up where they had left off and continuing their marriage, but the painful moments that he endured were still fresh in his mind. He remembered the countless times that he tried to convince her to stay, only to watch as she drifted farther away from him. He remembered the glimpses of hope that she provided along the way, when it looked like they would be able to repair their relationship, only to have things slip away each and every time. Sean was exhausted from riding this emotional roller-coaster. He was hopeful one moment and hopeless the next, and he knew that he didn't want to take the chance that this pattern would continue. His heart simply wasn't ready for that.

And then there was Blue Shirts. If he decided to take Jaclyn back, it certainly wouldn't be fair to her for him to continue working for the company. Although he didn't see himself staying with the company forever, he enjoyed the excitement, and sizable paycheck, that it provided. He also enjoyed reconnecting with Rob, as well as meeting the other men that worked for Anjelica, and he valued the camaraderie that they provided. Most importantly, Sean realized that Blue Shirts had restored his self-confidence, which had been slowly stripped away over the last six months. He felt like a man again, and the feeling was incredible.

As he drove back into his driveway, he was relieved to see that Jaclyn's car was gone, which spared him of having to have a conversation with her about where their relationship might now be headed. Once inside his kitchen, he poured himself another cup of coffee and collapsed into the brown leather couch in his living room. His house was empty, and he liked it that way.

Seventeen

Later that evening, Sean was standing inside the den of his parents' house, watching as his mother finished folding a blanket, eventually placing it on the back of the couch. Sean's father was sitting in his favorite chair, a gray cloth recliner that was situated in the corner of the room. They had recently finished dinner, and the house still smelled like pot roast and corn bread.

"Your father is feeling a lot better, or at least he thinks that he is," said Sean's mother.

Sean's mother was a kind and compassionate woman, with green eyes and long, strawberry blonde hair, mixed liberally with long streaks of gray. In her early 60s, she was in the closing years of a long career as a nurse who loved taking care of people. She had accompanied Jack to the doctor's office for his appointment earlier in the day, and was hopeful about the treatment options that the physician had given them. Jack's oncologist recommended removing the tumor with a lobectomy, a surgery that involved removing one of the lobes of his lung. The tumor itself was relatively small, but this procedure would ensure that it could be completely removed. The oncologist said that chemotherapy or radiation therapy would not be necessary prior to the surgery, which was scheduled for next week, however he said that there was a chance Jack might need one of those therapies after the procedure. He also assured Katherine that it looked like they had detected the cancer very early, and that Jack's long-term prognosis was promising.

"I'm as fit as a fiddle," Jack said, stifling a cough as he twisted uncomfortably in his recliner.

"Well, you definitely need your rest," said Sean, placing his hand on his father's shoulder. "And make sure to call me if you need anything at all."

"I'm going to be fine," Jack responded, as he slowly drifted off to sleep.

"Speaking of fine, how's the new job?" asked Katherine. "Jack mentioned that you were driving a taxi?"

"Not exactly," Sean replied. "It's more of a chauffer position, actually. I drive wealthy people around town, listen to their stories, take care of their needs. It's not all that different from what I did at Kenley & Logan, to be honest."

"Well, you're definitely your father's son," Katherine said, as she fluffed a pillow and placed it behind Jack's head. "It's not everyone who could bounce back the way you have, with Jaclyn, and your job, but you've managed to do it, and do it quite well. I know that he's proud of you - and so am I."

Sean smiled and hugged his mother, who gave him a covered dish of cherry cobbler to take home to Braden. As he left his parent's house, he was feeling a little guilty about receiving his mother's praise. The last few days had been a whirlwind, and he hadn't taken the time to think to reflect about his new job and new life, and how the two intertwined. He knew that he was essentially living a morally corrupt existence, and had surrounded himself with a circle of shady people doing shady things. Thinking about his mother made him feel ashamed of what he was doing, but he was also ashamed that he truly loved his new life, which was full of energy, excitement, money and power. Regardless, he wasn't ready to deal with these thoughts or emotions, as another hectic weekend was fast approaching. He reached for his cell phone and called Anjelica.

"I was wondering when you were going to call," purred Anjelica.

"Sorry, the day has just flown by so fast," Sean replied, as he maneuvered down a dark road on the outskirts of the county. "So tell me about the new client, 'Ms. Kincaid'? There wasn't a pickup time listed in the job alert. Is she still working out the details of her flight?"

"She's already here," Anjelica replied mischievously. "Her name is Avery

Kincaid. You met her at the party this past weekend. She's a sweet young lady and her mother is one of my oldest and dearest friends. She sent Avery to me so I could help educate her in the ways of the world, as her life to this point has been rather sheltered. Anyhow, she'll be staying at the house with me for a few weeks."

"I remember her," Sean said cautiously. "Young girl, dark hair. Right?"

"That's correct," replied Anjelica. "She took quite a shine to you at the party, and has been badgering me about you ever since. She's staying at the house with me, so just pick her up here at 10 a.m. on Friday. Her mother has purchased a standard 3-day package, so have her back to the house Monday morning."

"Sounds good, see you then," Sean replied.

The next morning, Sean was fast asleep when he heard his phone ringing. As his eyes opened, he could smell Jaclyn's fragrance on the pillow beside him from two nights before. He moved across his bed, answering the phone as he collapsed back onto his own pillow.

"Wake up, you big stud," said Rob sarcastically on the phone. "Ping just wrapped up his job and we're meeting him at Downpour in 20 minutes."

Sean lumbered out of bed, throwing on a pair of blue jeans, flannel shirt, and his favorite baseball cap, and made his way across town. As he approached Downpour, a coffee shop that was just a few miles east of the airport, he noticed Rob's truck in the small parking lot and parked beside it. Once inside, he saw Rob and Colby sitting at a table in the side of the shop. Rob sat his coffee down on the round, mosaic table and motioned to Sean. Colby was finishing a jelly donut and wiping the corners of his mouth with a paper napkin. Sean waved at his friends, and walked to the counter to order some coffee. A couple minutes later he was seated at the table with Rob and Colby.

"Ping just texted," Rob said, with a wry smile on his face. "He said he's running behind but he'll be here in a few minutes."

"I can't wait to get my truck back," Colby added, his voice muffled by the huge piece of pastry that was lodged in his jaw.

"So are you working this weekend?" Rob asked Sean.

"Yeah, it's Avery Kincaid," Sean responded. "Do you know her?"

"Uh oh," said both Rob and Colby in unison as they laughed and shook their heads. "Cling wrap," Colby added, as Rob nodded playfully.

"What's the matter?" asked Sean. "What do you mean by 'cling wrap'?"

"You know, 'cling wrap', clingy, whatever you want to call it," Rob responded. "Did you see the way that she was looking at you at Anjelica's? She's not looking for a roll in the hay - she's looking for a husband. You're going to have a hard time getting rid of that one."

"Anjelica said that Avery's mother sent her out here to learn about the 'ways of the world' or something like that," Sean countered.

"Avery's mother is Rose Kincaid," Rob replied. "You know, 'the burley baroness'? They made their money in tobacco and own half of the farms in North Carolina. The whole family is crazy. You're going to have your hands full with this one."

"Glad to hear," Sean said sarcastically.

Just then, the door swung open and Ping appeared. He saw Sean, Rob and Colby sitting at the table, gave them a slight wave, and began striding toward them. Although he appeared tired and disheveled, with his messy hair and his wrinkled blue dress shirt, which had come untucked and was dangling over his belt, Ping managed a smile for the men as he took a seat next to Sean.

"It's the man of the hour," Rob announced cheerfully. "So, how was it?"

"Good," Ping said, as he slid a set of car keys across the table to Colby.

"That's it?" Rob asked, this time more aggressively. "C'mon, we need more than just 'good.' We need details, man. Give us details."

"She was a nice lady," Ping responded coyly, which brought groans from Rob and Colby.

"Keep it up, Ping, and I'm not giving you a ride home," Colby said, bringing laughs from all of the men.

"Oh yeah, good point," said Ping, who burst out in laughter as well. "The lady was nice. She took me to dinner, took me dancing - I had a good time."

"You want some coffee?" Sean interjected, trying to spare Ping from having to answer Rob's insistent line of questioning.

"No thanks," Ping replied. "I'm going to bed soon. I don't need all that caffeine."

"So was she Asian?" Colby asked. "Why did she order Chinese take-out?"

"She was a white lady," Ping answered. "She didn't tell me her age but she was probably in her sixties. She said that she was getting ready to go on a 'girls trip' to Asia and that they would be visiting China, Thailand, Japan - and a couple other places over there that I can't remember right now. She had never traveled there before, so she asked Anjelica for a Blue Shirt that was Asian so she could 'immerse herself in Far East culture.' She kept asking me questions about Chinese history, Chinese people - stuff like that. She was fascinated with Chinese language too. She made me teach her a lot of words and phrases that she could use on her vacation."

"Did you sleep with her?" Rob asked brashly, after swallowing a gulp of coffee.

"Oh yes," Ping replied with a beaming smile. "We had a lot of sex. That's what she wanted to do the most."

All of the men laughed, and Colby rocked back in his chair, shaking his head.

"I got paid this morning too," Ping continued proudly. "I got a thousand dollar tip."

"Well done, my friend," Sean said, patting Ping on the back. "Did Anjelica say anything about sending you more work?"

"I spoke with her on the phone before I got here," Ping replied. "She said that I did a good job and she offered me a permanent position with the company."

"So what did you tell her?" Sean asked.

"I said 'hell yeah'," replied Ping, as the men again erupted in laughter. "This is fun. It's the best job I ever had."

Eighteen

On Friday morning, Sean stood on the front porch of Anjelica's house. After ringing the doorbell, he caught a glimpse of his reflection in one of the small windows located beside the large, oaken door. He tugged on the mustard-colored necktie that was layered across his blue dress shirt, which was hidden slightly beneath his dark gray sport coat. He ran his hand through his hair, swiping at some of his blonde locks to tuck them behind his left ear. The door opened, and Samson motioned for Sean to come inside.

"Good morning," Sean said to Samson, who was dressed similarly in a blue shirt and mustard-colored necktie. "Nice tie."

Samson rolled his eyes and left the foyer as Sean walked through the small corridor and into the living room. Standing there was Anjelica, dressed casually in a blue t-shirt and black yoga pants. Standing next to her was Avery, who was wearing a lavender blouse, white Capri pants, and purple heels.

"Sean, so good to see you again," Anjelica said as she hugged him and kissed him on the cheek. "You remember Avery, don't you?"

"How could I forget?" Sean replied, as he took Avery's hand and kissed it softly, which both surprised and delighted her. She giggled nervously as she lowered her head, looking awkwardly at Sean as he released her hand.

"You both are going to have an amazing time this weekend, I just know it," Anjelica shared, as she handed a white index card to Sean. "I've prepared a very basic itinerary for Avery, and everything that you need - times, addresses, et cetera

- is on that card. If you have any questions, just let me know."

Anjelica then turned to Avery, who was twirling the strands of her long, dark hair as she continued to smile like a schoolgirl at Sean.

"Oh dear, I seem to have left my favorite earrings upstairs," Anjelica continued, as her delicate fingers brushed against her ears. "Avery, would you mind getting them for me. They're the silver ones on my bedroom nightstand. And you might want to change your shoes too - it might be a little muddy this morning. Help yourself to any pair of flats that you can find in my closet."

"Oh, thank you," Avery responded, continuing to smile at Sean as she walked into the foyer. After she was sure that Avery had left the room, Anjelica moved closer to Sean and began to speak in a hushed tone.

"I'm guessing that Rob talked to you about Avery," Anjelica said. "What did he tell you?"

"Only that her mother is a tobacco heiress or something to that effect," Sean replied. "He really didn't say much beyond that."

"Rose Kincaid is a strong, independent woman, as well as one of my closest friends," continued Anjelica. "She was one of my first clients when I started Blue Shirts, and she was Rob's first assignment as well."

"He neglected to mention that," Sean said with a smile.

"Rose has been a widow for several years," shared Anjelica. "Her husband died shortly after they had Avery, which left quite a mark on them both. Rose was deeply in love with her husband, and his passing left her with an unbearable emptiness. Unfortunately at the time, Rose was more concerned with finding love again than raising Avery. She spent the next few years searching for love, but it was all in vain. She was unable to recapture the feeling that she had lost when she lost her husband. That's what led her to Blue Shirts."

"And along the way she lost touch with her daughter?" asked Sean.

"Sad, but true," replied Anjelica. "Rose wasn't much of a mother - she left the responsibilities of raising Avery to various nannies over the years, as well as a couple of relatives who didn't give a shit about her."

"So Avery became a typical rebellious teenager?" asked Sean.

"Quite the contrary," Anjelica replied. "The abandonment she felt from both her father and mother led Avery to be painfully shy and socially awkward, especially around members of the opposite sex. Growing up, Avery spent much of her childhood in boarding schools and summer camps, which gave her little opportunity to spread her wings. This has concerned her mother greatly. Rose is in fine health, but she's almost 70. She knows that she's not going to be around forever, and she would like Avery to find a nice man, fall in love and get married someday."

"Fall in love?" Sean asked innocently. "I don't think I'm her type."

"Not with you," Anjelica said, as she placed her hand on Sean's arm, "although I'm well aware that there's a chance that might happen. You're handsome and charming, and Avery is very young and impressionable. Granted, she's 31, but she is naïve in the ways of love. That's why Rose has instructed me to make sure that Avery loses her virginity during her stay here."

"I beg your pardon?" Sean asked quickly, as his eyes shifted across the room.

"She's a girl now, but Rose wishes her to be a woman when she returns to North Carolina," shared Anjelica.

"You know me," Sean continued with a wry smile. "Always happy to help."

"Fantastic," replied Anjelica. "Avery is staying here at the house, so you two may come and go as you please this weekend. Her flight leaves Monday morning, and her flight information is in the itinerary that I just gave you. Although her mother is footing the bill on this, I've created an official client profile for Avery and put the Blue Shirts app on her phone. I've also spoken to her about how much we value our privacy at the company, and for her to help us maintain this privacy by not speaking to anyone about us and what we do."

"Found them," Avery loudly announced as she walked back into the living room, holding a silver pair of earrings.

"Thank you, my dear," Anjelica said as she took the jewelry. "And I love the shoes. An excellent selection indeed."

Avery smiled and stuck her foot out towards Sean and Anjelica, proudly displaying the shoes that she found in Anjelica's closet.

"You two run along now," Anjelica said, as Sean and Avery began walking into the foyer toward the front door. "And don't do anything I wouldn't do!"

Just a few miles away, Detectives Wyatt and Miles were finishing their lunches at a table on the sidewalk a few blocks from the large courthouse that loomed over downtown Lexington. It was a bright and sunny day, and although it was the first day of April, the warm temperature made downtown seem more like June. The city was bustling with people who were enjoying the weather, many of whom were seated at tables on the sidewalk enjoying their lunches as well. Amidst the large crowd was a gathering of gray pigeons that were meandering about, searching for crumbs and other discarded food prizes.

"You promise?" Abby asked, after taking a sip of water from her Styrofoam cup. "You promise that this isn't an April Fools joke? Because if it is, it might be the best one you've ever pulled on me."

"It's the truth," Wyatt said, as he wadded up his napkin and placed it on his plate. "At least that's what Floss told me. Granted, he's a snake in the grass, but I don't think he's lying. He knows that I'll check out his story to make sure it's legit before even thinking about offering Dr. Luzzato a deal."

"A bordello that caters to women?" Abby asked with a slight chuckle. "Well, if this whole law enforcement thing doesn't work out for you, you might want to see if they're hiring."

"No thanks," Wyatt replied with a smile. "I can barely keep the one that I have at home happy."

"You realize that if this story is real, it's going to be a big deal around here?" Abby continued. "Have you ever even worked a case like this before?"

"Sort of," answered Wyatt. "We had a problem with massage parlors a few years before you joined vice. There were a handful scattered around the city, but then all of a sudden they started popping up everywhere. This pissed off the mayor, so he decided to make it a mission to run them all out of town. We ran surveillance, got the warrants that we needed, then went in and arrested the ladies that worked there - almost all of whom were either Korean or Filipino if I remember correctly. That was the last real action we had around here. You joined vice a little while after that, so you missed all the fun."

"Well, if all this is true, we might have our first real vice case in years," Abby said. "Have you spoken to anyone else about this at the station?"

"No, not yet," Wyatt responded, as he frowned and leaned back in his chair. "I don't see any reason to involve anyone else until I look into it a little more."

"Are you sure about that?" Abby asked, as she took another sip of water.

"This is personal," Wyatt replied. "I'm going to handle it myself."

"The hell you are," Abby replied, as she leaned toward Wyatt and placed her elbows on the table. "You know as well as I do that one cop can't do something like this alone. We're talking about surveillance, arrest warrants, computer forensics - need I go on?"

"Abby, I can't possibly get you involved in this," Wyatt replied.

"I've been working vice almost as long as you have," Abby continued, "and besides, "I'm already involved. I've been tailing Everett, and did an all-night stakeout at Anjelica Reardon's house in case you forgot. Besides, you know that you shouldn't work this alone. You need backup, as well as a second set of eyes on everything involved with this case. Otherwise, when you start making arrests, the D.A. will paint you as a rogue cop just looking to get revenge against Jack Everett's son. If he does that, the case won't even go to trial and all of your work will be down the drain."

Detective Wyatt continued to grimace as he listened to Abby.

"Look, I get it," Abby continued. "I know that you're still angry at Jack Everett for what he did to your father. But I don't want your anger towards him to cloud your judgment when dealing with his son, especially since it looks like he's involved with Anjelica Reardon. Face it, Tom - you need me."

"Fine, I give up," relented Wyatt, as he smiled in resignation at Abby.

"Good, then it's settled," replied Abby, who was smiling as well. "Glad to be working with you, Detective."

About thirty miles outside of town, a warm breeze was drifting across a beautiful farm just outside the county. Sean watched a pair of black horses that were frolicking behind a white wooden fence as he pulled into the driveway. As he parked beside a large black barn in the middle of the property, he turned to Avery, who was applying a generous amount of red lipstick while perched in the backseat.

"Where are we exactly?" asked Avery, as Sean opened the car door for her.

"It's a farm," Sean replied. "But it's not like one that you're probably accustomed to - here they raise horses instead of tobacco."

"It's incredible," Avery said, as she gazed at the majestic trees that hovered above them.

"It belongs to a friend of Anjelica's," Sean said, "but I don't think anyone is here right now. I suppose it would be alright if we explore the place. Shall we?"

Sean took Avery's hand and led her inside the barn, which smelled of fresh hay. As they walked inside, they immediately saw a row of stalls to their left and right. They heard a snort coming from the second stall on their right, followed by a loud sneeze that bellowed throughout the barn. As they approached, they saw a large horse, chestnut brown in color, turning effortlessly in its stall until its head was poking over the gate to greet them.

"He wants us to pet him," Avery said excitedly, as her fingers slid across the bridge of the horse's nose. A few seconds later, the horse nipped playfully at her wrist, which surprised her and caused her to giggle as she withdrew her hand.

"They like to be scratched behind their ears," Sean added. "Like this."

Sean began rubbing the horse behind his ear, as its big brown eyes began to flicker. As Avery began rubbing her hand behind his other ear, the horse began to nuzzle itself against her arm.

"What do you think his name is?" asked Avery.

"According to the sign it's 'Dollar Well Spent'," replied Sean, as he inspected the brass name plate that was attached to the wall of the stall. "He looks more like a thoroughbred than a quarter horse, so I'd say he's no stranger to the track."

"I want to go to the races, Sean," Avery interjected, clapping her hands excitedly. "Will you take me?"

"I would love to, but Keeneland doesn't start until next Friday," Sean responded. "How long are you in town for?"

"Oh, I'm in no rush to go back home," Avery replied. "Anjelica said that I could stay with her as long as I like."

"In that case, I don't see why not," said Sean, as he touched a brown leather bridle that was hanging on the wooden wall. "We'll just check with Anjelica when we get back and see if that's something we can schedule."

"Oh, thank you Sean," responded Avery. "It will be so much fun, especially since you know so much about horses. I bet there's so much that you could teach me."

"I don't know that much about them," Sean replied, "but when you grow up here, you realize that they're just as much a part of the community as you are. I know a few people in the horse business from my previous line of work though, so I've picked up a few things about them over the years."

"What did you used to do?" Avery inquired, as she turned toward Sean.

"I was a stockbroker up until just a few weeks ago," Sean responded. "Seems like a lifetime ago though."

"I still don't know what I want to do with my life," confided Avery. "Is that bad?"

"I wouldn't say that's 'bad', necessarily," responded Sean. "There's nothing wrong with taking your time and then deciding what path is best for you."

"My mother wants me to take over the family business," Avery continued, "but I don't think that I'm cut out for board rooms and conference calls. Honestly, I haven't worked a day in my life. It's embarrassing to say, but my mother has always taken care of me - she's always given me everything I've ever wanted or needed. She still sees me as a child and not as an adult. She doesn't think that I can take care of myself or make it on my own."

"Can you?" asked Sean, as he smiled and squeezed Avery's hand.

"No," said Avery, as she pouted, and then smiled, before moving closer to Sean. "But I will. Someday soon, I just know it."

Nineteen

It was now evening, and Sean and Avery were seated in Anjelica's living room. With his arm around Avery, Sean sipped from a glass of bourbon as she clung closely to him on the antique sofa. After slipping off her heels, she curled her legs up onto the sofa, leaning closely against Sean as he took a long drink from his glass.

They had spent the early part of the afternoon at the farm, wandering around and looking at other barns and rustic buildings that were scattered about the property. Later that afternoon, Sean took her shopping in downtown Lexington, stopping into a couple of the boutiques that Anjelica had suggested in her itinerary. Later, they had an extravagant dinner at a secluded Italian restaurant in the southern part of the city. Avery was enchanted by the candlelight, as well as the music from the violinist who was performing Mozart in the corner of the restaurant. She enjoyed a couple of large glasses of Merlot - the first of which made her giggly and the second a bit more spontaneous and much less reserved.

It had become apparent to Sean that Avery was now very comfortable with him. She was shy and quiet around him when the day began, but now she was very much at ease in his company. Over the course of the day, she had become talkative and engaging, and on a number of occasions she tried her hand at flirting with him. As she sat on the sofa next to him, Sean noticed that Avery's eyes were almost always fixed upon him - a deep, loving stare that Sean knew all to well. He had seen this look many times in his life, from the various girls who had fallen for him during his nights at the Speakeasy, to the countless times that Jaclyn gazed into his eyes during the course of their marriage. He knew that Avery had fallen for him.

As she nuzzled against him and softly kissed his neck, Sean ran his hand through the back of her hair and looked across the room at the portrait of Belle Brezing hanging on the wall. As he stared at the painting, he contemplated the contents of the safe that was hidden behind it.

"You two certainly look like you're enjoying yourselves," announced Anjelica, as she entered the living room from the kitchen holding a pair of wine glasses. She was barefoot and wearing only a blue, long-sleeved shirt and white pajama bottoms as she approached her houseguests. She handed Avery one of the glasses of wine and sat on the sofa across from them.

"Today was amazing," Avery said, slurring her speech slightly as she took a sip of the red wine that Anjelica had brought her. "Sean is amazing too," she continued, as she kissed him on the mouth. As Avery kissed him, Sean was slightly embarrassed with the lingering display of affection taking place in front of Anjelica. He pulled away slightly from Avery and smiled awkwardly at his hostess, who was curled up on her sofa as she caressed her wine glass.

"Sorry," Avery said to Anjelica, "I just get carried away sometimes."

"Don't mind me," replied Anjelica with a devilish smile, as a strand of her long, dark hair fell across her face. "I like a good show every now and then."

"So, Avery says she's going to be staying here for a while?" Sean interjected nervously.

"I want to go to the races next weekend!" exclaimed Avery, as she rose slightly from her seat. "Can Sean take me? Please?"

"I don't see why not," replied Anjelica, as she brushed the fallen strand of hair behind her ear with her hand. "Are you available, Sean?"

"I would be delighted," he replied, as Avery clapped her hands and hugged him.

"Fantastic," said Anjelica. "I'll make all of the arrangements. We're actually having several of our ladies in town, with it being opening weekend at Keeneland

and all. We're planning an outing there on Saturday and it should be quite the affair."

"I can't believe that I get you all to myself again next weekend," Avery added excitedly.

"I can't believe it either," Sean said, as he grinned politely and took the last drink of his bourbon.

"Oh my, would you look at the time?" Anjelica said, as she glanced at the antique grandfather clock in the corner of the room. "I have a big day tomorrow, so if you'll excuse me I'm going to head upstairs to bed. Is there anything that you need before I turn in?"

"I have everything that I need right here," Avery said sweetly as she squeezed Sean.

"Perfect," Anjelica replied. "Good night, you two. See you in the morning."

Anjelica rose from her sofa, hugged Sean and Avery, kissed them on their cheeks, and exited through the foyer. As soon as she disappeared from view, the room became quiet. Sean held Avery as she nuzzled her head into his neck and continued to embrace him firmly. He sat his drink down on the table next to the sofa and ran his fingertips against the back of her dress.

"Would you like another drink?" he asked.

"No thank you," she replied, as she tried to stifle a yawn. "I'm not much of a drinker. I've probably had more wine tonight than I've ever had in my entire life. It's sad, right?"

"Of course not," Sean replied, as he caressed her cheek with his hand. "If anything it's admirable that you don't need alcohol to have a good time."

"Are you staying the night?" asked Avery, abruptly changing the subject as she lowered her head and looked at Sean from the corner of her eye.

"I'd planned on it," Sean responded. "I can crash down here, or take one of the extra bedrooms. Or I could stay with you in your room if you like."

"I'd like that," replied Avery slowly, with a nervous smile. "Should we go upstairs now?"

"We can go whenever you like," Sean responded.

"I'm ready," Avery replied, as she stood up and looked at Sean, who lifted himself off of the sofa, took her hand, and began walking towards the foyer. There were no words as they ascended the staircase, and then walked through the upstairs hallway.

As they entered Avery's room, which was located next to the master bedroom, Sean turned on the light switch. The room smelled like perfume, and was heavily decorated with a rustic, equine theme. The walls were covered in faded, pink wallpaper, and pictures of horses in wooden frames were hung throughout the room. There were shelves that surrounded the room from the ceiling above. The shelves housed a large collection of books, mostly about horses, farms, and local history. Near the doorway was a white dresser, the top covered by Avery's purple suitcase and some clothing that was scattered about. Across the room was a day bed, covered in quilts and pillows, nestled in the corner of the room underneath a window that was covered by a thin, white chiffon drapery.

Avery turned off the light switch and moved toward the bed, and the room was almost completely dark, except for the streetlight penetrating the curtain that covered the window. She peeled back the quilts and sheets, climbed into the bed, and then quickly pulled them back over her body until they reached her neck. With most of her body hidden beneath the covers, Sean watched as Avery fumbled with her clothes underneath the blankets, removing each article of her clothing and placing them on the nightstand beside the bed. Soon, she was completely naked, albeit behind a layer of quilts and sheets that obscured her body below her shoulders. While holding the top of her blanket tightly, she stared at Sean as he stood silently next to the bed.

Sean began to undress - first removing his necktie, folding it and placing it on the night stand. He unbuttoned his blue dress shirt, all the while maintaining eye contact with Avery, and then he placed it next to his tie. He watched as she studied the muscular contours of his chest, his arms, and his stomach. Next, he removed his shoes and socks, and slid them next to the night stand with his feet. Finally, he unbuckled his belt, unbuttoned his pants, and let them fall to the floor. Finally, Sean slid off his gray boxer briefs, as he continued to stare at Avery. Her mouth opened slightly as she stared at Sean's manhood before her eyes returned to his face. Sean pulled back the covers and crawled into bed next to Avery, whose body was trembling slightly as he settled in next to her. With his hand, he touched her face and kissed her tenderly on the lips.

"I'm scared, Sean," confessed Avery in a low whisper. "I've never been with a man before and I'm afraid that I won't know what to do."

"How about you just relax," replied Sean, "and let me do all the work?"

Avery nodded nervously as Sean kissed her again and slid his hand beneath the covers, gliding it gracefully across her breasts and stomach. As he pulled away from her mouth, Sean stared at her deeply as he moved his hand below her waist, which tickled her and made her smile. Sean then placed his fingertips inside her, which caused Avery's body to shudder. She sighed loudly, and then found herself struggling to breathe as Sean continued to explore her body. She ran her hand through Sean's hair while he kissed her breasts, breathless with excitement as he slowly maneuvered his way beneath the covers until he was kissing her stomach. Avery squeezed both of Sean's hands tightly, her fingers interlocking with his, as he softly kissed her thighs.

Avery couldn't believe what was happening, and how incredible Sean made her feel. Her body was writhing in ecstasy, but these feelings were overwhelming and very new to her. With trepidation, she looked down at Sean while he continued to pleasure her, and marveled at how his blonde hair glistened in the light that was streaming through the window. Suddenly, Sean looked up to find Avery watching him, which made her nervously look away. Her eyes darted quickly around the shadowy room until they landed on a portrait of a horse that was hanging on the wall just above the bed. She stared at the picture as she felt the tingling throughout her body grow stronger. She lifted her head off of her pillow to look down at Sean again, until she felt her body shudder uncontrollably. She arched her back, fell backwards into the bed, and let out a passionate scream that resonated loudly throughout the bedroom.

Sean slowly crawled up Avery's trembling body until he was now on top of her. Breathlessly, she kissed him as he ran his hand over her long, brown hair, some of which was covering her face.

"Are you okay?" he asked, as he ran his thumb softly over her chin.

"Oh...my...God," she responded, drawing out each word individually to emphasize how good Sean had made her feel.

Sean smiled and kissed Avery, and then he moved his hips toward hers, slowly and carefully, until he was inside her. At first she was motionless beneath him, but as he began to move back and forth within her, he felt her body grinding against his body until they were in perfect rhythm. Avery continued to cry out with each thrust, each moan louder than the next. She closed her eyes tightly shut, and squeezed the back of Sean's neck with her left hand while she dug the fingernails of her right hand deeply into the cotton sheets. At one point Sean looked up and saw his reflection in the glass of the window above the bed. He looked at himself, pondering for a moment on what he was doing. Yes, this was business, but he knew that he should feel guilty about taking Avery's virginity, even though it had been arranged by her mother. Even more troublesome to Sean was that he didn't feel guilty about it. He didn't feel encumbered by his feelings from his dalliance with Stella, who was mature and experienced, but he knew that making love to Avery now would likely change her profoundly as a person. Still, he continued, without reservation, to bring the young woman pleasure that she had never known.

Both exhausted and excited, Avery eventually drifted off to sleep after making love to Sean for the better part of the evening. As with the previous weekend, he found it difficult to sleep in the strange bed, which was much smaller than what he was accustomed to - especially with Avery curled up beside him. He was thirsty, so he got up, put on his underwear, and made his way down the hallway. As he passed by the door of Anjelica's bedroom - which was now open - he heard a familiar voice from within whisper loudly to him.

"Mission accomplished?" Anjelica asked, while sitting up in her bed. She was wearing reading glasses and had a book in her lap.

"A gentleman does not kiss and tell," Sean replied coyly, as he entered Anjelica's bedroom.

"Oh, honey, you're not telling me anything that I don't already know," Anjelica responded playfully. "Why do you think I'm awake right now? I couldn't sleep a wink with her in the next room screaming bloody murder."

"Sorry," Sean replied as he smiled and lowered his head.

"Nothing to be sorry about," said Anjelica, as she patted the side of the bed.

Sean sat down on the edge of her large, king-sized bed, brushing up against one of her knees, which was tangled beneath the covers. Anjelica's bedroom was beautifully decorated, with gold-colored furniture placed perfectly throughout the room. The bed itself featured a large white headboard that was trimmed in gold and stretched halfway up to the ceiling. Her bed was flanked by a pair of gold end tables, each with an antique lamp that was softly lighting the room. She reached for a bottle of water that was resting on the end table next to her and handed it to Sean. He opened it, took a drink, and handed it back to her.

"How is next weekend going to work exactly?" asked Sean. "I'm just wondering because next week is my son's spring break. I have him all of next week, so I didn't know exactly when you would need me."

"Ah, yes, I forgot that you were a family man," replied Anjelica condescendingly, as she took a drink from the water bottle.

"His mother is bringing him to me on Monday morning," Sean replied, "and I have him all the way until Friday. Is that okay?"

"That's fine," answered Anjelica. "Avery is supposed to have you until Monday morning, but let's plan on sending you home Sunday evening. I'll speak with her and she should be fine with that, especially since she'll be getting you next weekend. Spend the week with your son, and then on Friday night you can come by the house and start your next assignment with Avery. That way your son can see his Daddy next week and Avery can call you 'Daddy' all weekend. Sound good?"

"Wow. Yes, I appreciate it," Sean said gratefully. "Thank you."

"See, I'm not such a bitch, now am I?" asked Anjelica playfully. "Now kiss me goodnight and go back to taking care of our little houseguest in the room next door."

Sean leaned over towards Anjelica, planting a light kiss on her mouth. As he began to pull away, she pulled him closer and kissed him deeply, placing both of her hands on his face. Sean closed his eyes and felt her tongue moving inside his mouth. When he opened his eyes, he noticed that her eyes were open as well, and that she had been staring at him the entire time through her reading glasses. As he drew away from her, he stood up and began to walk towards the doorway.

"You didn't ask me if there was anything that I wanted in return," Anjelica said just before Sean left the room. With his back to Anjelica, Sean looked over his shoulder and then turned to face her. "You know - for helping you out with next week's schedule."

"Forgive me," Sean said. "Is there anything that you have in mind?"

Anjelica smiled and pointed at the bulge in the front of Sean's underwear.

"I see," Sean said, with a boyish smile.

"April is dreadfully busy," Anjelica replied, "but after the Kentucky Derby, the rest of May generally slows down a bit. When that time comes, I'll arrange to have you spend a weekend with me as my own personal Blue Shirt. This way I can try out the merchandise and see what all of the fuss is about. Is that understood?"

"Understood," replied Sean, as his smile grew wider.

Twenty

It was very early on Monday morning, and Sean was at a Starbucks drive-thru ordering a large coffee with a shot of espresso. He had just left Anjelica's house after saying goodbye to Avery, who lingered on the front porch to watch him drive away. They had spent most of the weekend making love in Avery's bedroom, with the one exception being when they took in a movie downtown at the historic theatre just a few streets away from the house. They spent most of the weekend alone, as Anjelica had decided to go to Chicago for a last-minute trip with some of her girlfriends. As he took a drink of his coffee, his mind flashed back to the sight of Avery watching him as he drove away. She was beyond smitten with him, and appeared forlorn as he drove away, like a puppy dog waiting for her master to return. It was something that was becoming more difficult for him to ignore.

After picking up Braden from Jaclyn's house, Sean began to feel normal again. It had seemed like an eternity since he had seen Braden, and he was looking forward to a quiet day at the house with him. A familiar alert sounded on Sean's phone, followed quickly by another beep. As they pulled into the garage of their house, Braden jumped out of the truck and headed upstairs.

"I'll be up in a minute," Sean said, as he opened the hatch and grabbed the overnight bag that he had been keeping in the rear of his truck. The light from the screen of the phone glowed eerily in the darkness of the basement as Sean walked towards the stairs. Once inside his kitchen, Sean set his bag on the counter and took a long drink of his coffee while Braden pulled a packet of bacon and a carton of eggs out of the refrigerator.

"I'm making breakfast," Braden announced proudly. "How many eggs do you want, Dad?"

"Thanks, son," replied Sean. "I'll do two."

"How about three?" Braden responded. "Mom says you look like H-E-L-L and could stand to put some meat on your bones."

"Three it is," said Sean with a smile, relenting to his son's request.

As Braden turned on the stove and removed the skillets from a nearby cabinet, Sean took a seat at the counter and began looking at his phone. He saw an email confirming that he had just received a Paypal deposit of $8,000, which brought a smile to his face that he obscured from Braden by taking a long drink from his coffee cup. After opening his Blue Shirts app, he looked at his most recent client receipt and saw that he had indeed received a $3,000 tip from Avery's mother, Rose Kincaid. He also noticed that he had received a new job alert for this coming weekend, which as expected was for Avery. He was delighted to see that he wasn't needed at Anjelica's house until 7 p.m. on Friday evening, and he would have all week to spend with his son.

Sean spent all week with Braden, and they took a trip to the mall, had dinner at some of their favorite restaurants, and on a particularly warm day, paid a visit to a driving range to hit a few buckets of golf balls. On Wednesday afternoon, Sean took his son and his parents to Cincinnati for opening day of the baseball season. Jack and Katherine were happy to see their grandson, and Sean was excited to see that his father was looking much better, having regained a lot of the color he had lost over the last few weeks. While decked out in his Cincinnati Reds jersey, Braden devoured almost every stadium food he could find - from hot dogs to pretzels to a large slice of pizza, washing it all down with several gulps of his root beer. The Reds won, and as a series of fireworks exploded in the sky above the stadium, Sean felt thankful - and grateful - that his family was together to enjoy this wonderful experience.

The following day, Sean slept in for most of the morning, until Braden woke him up at noon so they could play catch in their backyard. Later that evening, Braden had a couple of friends over to play video games while Sean did laundry, ran a load of dishes and paid bills. While his son was downstairs with his friends,

Sean sat on the couch with a bottle of Corona and balanced his checkbook. He was relieved to see how the income from his new job was making such a big difference in his life. Even after writing checks for his house payment, truck payment, and other assorted bills, he had more money in his account than he had at any time over the past few months.

He checked his phone and saw that he had received texts from Ping and Rob.

"You working this weekend?" asked Ping in his text. "I'm taking a lady to Keeneland and don't know shit about it. Call me."

"Go to a gas station and buy the Daily Racing Form," Sean texted back. "Study it tonight and I'll call you tomorrow."

Sean then began putting away his checkbook and receipts, and grabbed a box of Wheat Thins from his kitchen pantry. He took a long sip of his beer and looked at Rob's text.

"I hear you're practically a married man now LOL," said Rob in his text. "Where do I send the wedding gift?"

"F.U. :-)," Sean texted back as he stifled a laugh and threw a couple of crackers into his mouth.

"Is that any way to talk to your best man?" Rob texted back.

"Asshole," typed Sean in his reply, now laughing even harder, as he took another long sip of beer before emphatically hitting 'send' on his phone to deliver his reply.

"Gotta go," Rob responded a couple minutes later. "See you this weekend."

On Friday morning, Sean took Braden with him as they ran errands. After stopping for breakfast, they went to the post office and later to the dry cleaners, where Sean picked up another batch of blue dress shirts. Braden took the shirts from his father and hung them on the hook next to the seat directly behind Sean.

"Why do they make you wear blue shirts?" Braden asked. "Does it have anything to do with the Wildcats?"

"I don't think so," answered Sean, as he squinted his eyes and flipped down the sun visor on his truck. "It's just our uniform, that's all. The color blue is meant to convey 'trust', so I would imagine that the company chose blue because our clients are entrusting us to make sure they get to places safely."

"Mom says that chauffeurs don't make a lot of money," added Braden, "and that all you do is sit in your car all day."

"Actually, it pays pretty well," Sean replied, with a smirk on his face. "And if your mother ever watched me do my job, it would make her head spin."

Later that afternoon, after dropping Braden off at Jaclyn's, Sean returned home to begin getting dressed for the evening. He picked out a light blue necktie from his closet and placed it across his dark blue dress shirt, tying it quickly and pulling it snug against his neck. He ran a lint roller across his dark gray slacks, and slipped his feet into the dark black loafers that were resting near the bottom of his dresser. He lifted the collar of his shirt and sprayed a small mist of cologne onto his chest, and then studied himself in the full-length cherry-trimmed mirror in the corner of his bedroom.

Just before he was getting ready to leave, his phone rang. As Sean began to answer it, he could see that it was Ping calling him.

"You gonna tell me about horses or not?" asked Ping, who sounded like he was on the verge of panic. "I read the Racing Form and I still don't know what the hell is going on."

"So you don't know anything about horse racing?" Sean asked, as he walked from the bedroom into his kitchen to inspect the contents of the laundry basket that was resting on the counter.

"I know that I'm about the same size as the guys who ride them," Ping replied with a chuckle.

"So you've never been to Keeneland?" asked Sean, as he fished a dark blue dress sock out of the laundry basket.

"No, that's 'white people' fun," Ping responded with another snicker. "I'm Chinese, remember?"

"Okay, okay," Sean said, as he started laughing along with Ping, while he plucked another blue sock out of the basket. "Here's the deal - your client will probably know enough about horses and betting. But if she does happen to ask you for any tips, tell her to bet on the jockeys more than the horses. A lot of people don't know this, but the top ten jockeys in the standings win about 90 percent of the races. If all else fails or you get flustered, just ask me or Rob for help that day and we'll feed you information."

"Okay," Ping replied. "So you'll definitely be there?"

"Yeah, I'm pretty sure," answered Sean. "Anjelica made it sound like it's a company thing. Lots of clients, lots of Blue Shirts - you get the picture."

A little over an hour later, Sean pulled up to Anjelica's house, parked on the street, and began to make the familiar walk down her sidewalk. As he neared her yard, the front door flew open and Avery came running out.

"Sean!" she cried out as she ran to him and hugged him tightly. "I missed you."

"I missed you too," he replied, wondering if she had any idea that he didn't mean it.

"It's been the longest week of my life," she continued, almost frantically. "Not being able to see you, or call you - I didn't know what to do with myself."

"Well, you don't have to worry about that now, do you?" Sean said with a smile and soothing voice. "You have me all weekend."

"I do! I do!" she exclaimed, as she pulled him inside the house and into the foyer. From there, Avery quickly brought Sean upstairs to her bedroom, which looked exactly as it did the weekend before. Avery, who was wearing a black cocktail dress and white pearls, closed the door of her room and began kissing Sean quickly and passionately.

"We have to hurry," she said, as she unbuckled his belt, pulled down his slacks, and sank to her knees, all within a matter of seconds. "We have theatre tickets for 8 p.m."

An hour later, while sitting in a darkened concert hall next to Avery, Sean watched as the actors and actresses glided gracefully across the stage. It was a touring production of Les Miserables, a musical that Sean had seen with Jaclyn almost ten years ago in this very building. As Avery squeezed his hand, Sean listened as the performers sang passionately about love, loss, forgiveness, and redemption. He was particularly moved by the character of Jean Valjean, an honorable man who had broken the law by stealing bread to feed his starving family. Sean identified with Valjean, and felt as if he could truly understand his plight. Sean was also affected by the character of Javert, the lawman who doggedly pursues Valjean throughout the story. Sean hadn't given much thought to the illegal aspect of his new job, but he was reminded of it by the story that was unfolding on stage before him. As he watched the show's dramatic conclusion, he began to wonder if he would ever encounter a "Javert" of his own who was determined to bring him to justice. And if so, he contemplated what he would do, what he would say, and how he would act. As the show ended to a thunderous array of applause, Sean stood up with the rest of the audience and clapped for the actors as they took their final bows.

It was now Saturday morning, and Sean walked out of one of Anjelica's guest bathrooms after taking a brief shower. As he trod down the hallway wearing only a white towel, he noticed that the house was abuzz with activity. He looked down over the handrail and into the foyer and caught a glimpse of several men and women milling about. He ducked into Avery's bedroom and saw her standing in front of a mirror in a black skirt, pink blouse, and a large, flowery hat.

"Oh, there you are," she said. "You better get dressed - the bus is here."

"The bus?" asked Sean.

Sean got dressed quickly, slipping on a pair of black, pinstriped pants and the freshly-laundered blue dress shirt that was hanging on the hinge of the mirror. A few minutes later, Sean and Avery walked briskly downstairs and out the front door. On the lawn were Rob, Colby and Ping, all dressed in blue shirts, dark suit jackets, black slacks, and shiny, black shoes. Just behind the men, parked on the street in front of the house, was a large transport bus. It was large and very sleek, with metallic black paint, gold trim, and gray tinted windows.

"So what do you think?" Rob asked as he glanced back at the large, shiny vehicle and then looked back at Sean.

"It's the party bus!" cackled Ping excitedly. "It's time to party!"

Sean and Avery walked onto the grass and followed the men through the yard towards the bus. The door was open, and the men waited for Avery to enter first. Sean held Avery's hand as she climbed the large set of steps that led into the vehicle, followed by Sean and the rest of the guys. As he looked inside, he nodded at the driver, who was an older man wearing a maroon colored shirt. As he turned the corner and entered the cabin of the vehicle, he was met by the sight of a large group - perhaps 30 or so - of men and women gathered inside. The interior of the bus was luxurious and extravagant, featuring two long, curving rows of black leather seats that snaked their way along its walls. He also noticed two television screens that were mounted in the corners of the ceiling behind him, as well as two fully stocked bars that protruded from each row of seats. Towards the rear of the bus, obscured somewhat by a small throng of people that had congregated in the center of the vehicle, was a long, silver pole that stretched from the floor to the ceiling.

"What's the matter?" Colby asked Sean, as he smiled and brushed up against him. "Ain't you ever been in a bus with a stripper pole before?"

"Okay, is that everyone?" shouted Anjelica, who entered the vehicle and was standing next to the driver. "Can everybody hear me?" she shouted again, as the people within continued to mutter and mill about the cabin. She smiled, and took a microphone that the driver handed her and spoke again.

"Can everyone hear me?" she asked again, this time with her voice booming through the speakers of the bus' sound system. The guests aboard the bus responded with a round of cheers for their hostess as she took a quick sip from the straw of the large plastic cup she was holding.

"I hope you don't mind, but I took the liberty of procuring a bus to take us to Keeneland today," she continued, which brought about an even louder roar of approval from the people on board. "Just have a drink, relax, and enjoy yourselves. I sure as hell plan to. Cheers!"

Anjelica raised her cup, as did most of the guests on board. The door of the bus closed as its engine began rumbling. She approached Sean and Avery, who had both already taken their seats, leaning over to give them both a hug and a kiss on the cheek. As Anjelica migrated toward the rear of the vehicle, the bus slowly pulled out into the street.

"What are you drinking?" asked a familiar voice from a few feet away. Sean looked over to see Raoul standing by one of the bars, scooping an empty glass into a cooler of crushed ice.

"Woodford," Sean replied before turning to Avery. "And you?"

"The same," she said, as she ran her hand across Sean's thigh.

"Are you sure?" asked Sean. "Have you ever had bourbon before? It can have quite a kick to it if you're not careful."

"I'll be fine," she responded.

"Two Woodfords then," Sean said to Raoul, "but put Coke in hers. Lots of it."

"You have to admire a lady who knows what she wants," Raoul added, as he smiled and handed them their drinks. "Am I right, amigo?"

The driver turned on the stereo, and music filled the air of the bus. A couple of the ladies on board took off their shoes and began dancing on the light gray carpet that lined the aisles next to the seats. As everyone continued to laugh and mingle, Sean took a drink of his bourbon and began stroking Avery's back as she took a sip of her drink and wrinkled her nose. As he glanced around the bus, he looked across the aisle to see Ping and Rob sitting with their dates. Ping raised his glass and smiled at Sean, who returned the gesture and raised his glass as well. Ping appeared to be in a particularly good mood, as he had been paired with an attractive client who appeared to be in her early 50s. The woman was a short brunette with long, curly dark hair and a dark complexion, and she looked to be of either Hispanic or Italian descent. Ping raised his eyebrows and smiled at Sean, as he playfully rolled his eyes around in his head. It was obvious that Ping found her to be very pretty, and he was right. She had an exotic look to her - especially her eyes, which were dark, mysterious and beautiful.

Rob's date was much older, perhaps in her early sixties, and had long auburn hair sprinkled with a few blonde highlights. She was pretty, but you could tell by her face that she had no doubt had some work done. Her lips were unusually large and puffy, and her eyes were pulled tightly across her skin. The woman was tall, and wearing a beautiful salmon colored dress with a dressy hat to match. Both women seemed comfortable, and acted like they had known each other for quite some time. Sean watched as Rob and Ping charmed the women. He had seen Rob do it hundreds of times before, but watching Ping operate was an entirely different experience. Sean watched and listened as Ping interacted with his date, observing his style, his delivery, and most importantly, his ability to listen. After all, whether you were entertaining a woman for just a short time or even a lifetime, that was the key. It's what Rob had taught him to do many years ago, and it's what Ping was doing now in masterful fashion.

Sean glanced down the aisles to see if there was anyone else on board that he might recognize. Of course there was Raoul, who was still playing bartender for everyone as he swayed along with the music, and next to him was Derek, the pilot from Las Vegas that Sean had also met previously at Anjelica's house. Raoul's date had big blue eyes and even bigger blonde hair, and was decked out in a colorful pastel pantsuit with a hat decorated in chiffon and lace. Derek's date was standing next to him, nodding along as she followed a story that he was telling to a small group of guests that were gathered around him. Derek's client had short dark hair, a toothy smile, and a bright red blouse, and she appeared to be hanging on his every word.

To Derek's left was Colby, who was paired with a woman who was apparently new to the group, as she kept introducing herself as "Diane" to the men and women who were scattered about the bus. She was in her forties, had short blonde hair, and was wearing a beige blouse and a pair of denim blue jeans. At one point she burst into laughter when Colby took her hand and insisted that she rub his bald head. Just then, Samson emerged from a small bathroom located in the rear of the bus, and stood next to Colby while Diane finished rubbing his head. Colby then pulled Diane's hand off of his own head and placed it on Samson's bald head. As she rubbed his head, everyone in the group began to laugh, including Samson, who bent down and leaned towards her so she could reach him easier. This also seemed to please the tall woman who approached Samson and began rubbing one of his arms. She was in her late forties, with short blonde hair, and was wearing a green short-sleeved shirt, white pants, and appeared to be Samson's date for today's excursion. Sean also noticed that she had a distinctive Irish accent, which seemed to project throughout the bus.

There were also several other men on the bus, all of whom obviously were Blue Shirts as evidenced by their attire. Sean recognized a few of them from the party he had attended at Anjelica's house, although he hadn't been introduced to them. He watched as they all attended to their clients - stroking their arms, complimenting them incessantly, laughing at their jokes. It was fascinating to watch.

Of the remaining clients in the group, Sean didn't recognize any of them from the party. He enjoyed watching them - intrigued by not just their appearances, but by the way they carried themselves. Yes, most of the women shared the same physical traits - beautiful faces, expensive hairstyles, and long, slender bodies. And yes, most of them dressed similarly too, with their fashionable clothes, gaudy jewelry and expensive shoes - but they all seemed to have a certain grace about them. There was an air they projected that was indicative of wealth, sophistication and privilege. Sean was familiar with these types of people from his days as a stockbroker, as many of his clients were either rich or thought they were rich. There was a time not long ago when he was well on his way to entering that stratosphere, back when he was making a very good living as a young hotshot with Kenley & Logan. He wanted that life, and he spent many years working hard so that he and his family could one day be a part of that life, but it was not to be. He was still bitter about losing his job and losing his wife, but as he looked at the faces of the people inside the bus, he realized that he had been given another opportunity for the life that he had dreamt of and worked for - and he could have a lot of fun along the way.

"Ladies and gentlemen, we've arrived," announced Anjelica over the intercom, which drew cheers from her guests. "Follow me!"

It was a warm, sunny day at Keeneland, and thousands of people poured into the grandstand to watch the races. Sean took Avery's hand as they stepped off the bus and joined the rest of the group, following Anjelica into a side entrance of the facility. Once they arrived inside, Avery marveled at the large crowds milling about, consisting primarily of well-dressed men and women in expensive clothes and interesting-looking hats. She was also taken with the enormity of the oval track, stretching over a mile long, as well as the giant scoreboard that was perched atop the lush, perfectly-manicured green grass that comprised the infield of the racetrack.

With Anjelica directing traffic in the aisle, she ushered Sean and Avery into a small row of seats not far from the railing of the track. To Sean's right were Ping and his date, who was fidgeting with a sparkly purse that was resting in her lap. To Sean's left were Avery, who seemed to be a little tipsy from the drink that she had on the bus, and to her left were Rob and Colby, as well as their dates, both of whom were engaged in a deep conversation.

"Even the dirt is pretty!" Avery exclaimed from her seat, as the men in the row laughed.

"The dirt contains sand, silt and clay," remarked Ping, who leaned over towards Avery from his seat next to Sean. "They just redid it a few months ago to help with the drainage."

Ping's date smiled proudly at him, as did Rob and Colby, who turned to each other and nodded impressively. Sean turned to Ping as well, sporting a perplexed look on his face.

"Wow, you sure know a lot about horse racing," replied Avery, while Ping nodded, smiled and leaned over slowly towards Sean.

"I read about it in the Daily Racing Form," Ping whispered in Sean's ear, causing him to shake his head and laugh.

"By the way, I'm Elena," said Ping's date, leaning over him to shake Sean's hand.

"Pleased to meet you," Sean replied. "I'm Sean, and this is Avery." Avery waived politely to Elena and then retracted in her seat, quickly placing her hand on Sean's thigh with territorial jealously.

"Where are my manners?" Rob asked, as he pivoted sharply in his seat. "This lovely young lady is Patricia, and this other wonderful young lady is Diane. Diane gets the honor of putting up with Colby all day."

"I resent that remark," announced Colby, feigning both surprise and disrespect, which drew laughs from the row. Rob introduced Sean and Avery to the women as well, and that seemed to perk Avery back up.

"It's a pleasure," said Patricia, who waived and smiled at both Sean and Avery. "It's simply gorgeous today, isn't it?"

"It certainly is," replied Sean, trying his best not to stare at her oversized lips and other artificially-enhanced features. "You couldn't ask for a better day."

"Ah, Avery," Rob said, as he took Avery's hand and kissed it gently. "You look spectacular as always. So good to see you again, and please tell your mother I said 'hello'."

"Thank you Rob," gushed Avery. "I'll certainly give her your best."

"It won't be the first time," Rob added coyly, which drew a smattering of laughs from the rest of the group, as well a playful smack on the shoulder from Patricia.

"I don't understand," replied Avery in confusion.

"Oh, quit teasin' my girl," Diane said to Rob, with a thick, southern twang. "Good to meet you both," she added as she smiled at Sean and Avery, who nodded back with a slight grin on her face.

"I'll be right back, I need to go to the restroom," Avery said as she turned to Sean. "Do you know where it is?"

"It's just up the stairs and on the right," answered Sean. "Would you like me to come with you?"

"Oh no, I'll be fine," replied Avery. "I want to stretch my legs for a minute anyway and get a good look at this place. I'll bring back a couple of drinks too if you like. Woodford, right?"

"That's right," Sean replied, "but you might want to slow down a bit. I think that first one's hitting you kind of hard."

"Oh, nonsense, you silly boy," said Avery as she playfully squeezed Sean's chin and pulled him closer to her. "I won't be gone long. Will you miss me?"

"Desperately," replied Sean, as he forced a smile and kissed her quickly on the lips.

Avery walked up the steps within the grandstand, pausing for a moment to watch the lines forming in front of the wall of betting windows. She saw a group of young men, perhaps college age, smoking cigars and wearing fedoras. Their necks were craned toward a large television that hung from a nearby wall. Avery slowly walked by the men, hoping that one of them would notice her, but they continued to fix their attentions on the screen above. She pouted slightly then entered the restroom.

At his trackside seat, Sean watched as Anjelica continued to mingle with her clients, floating from one row to the next to attend to their needs. He looked over and saw that Rob had just plopped down into Avery's empty seat. He pulled a silver flask out of his jacket pocket, unscrewed it, sighed, and took a drink.

"So what do you think?" asked Rob, as he handed Sean the flask.

"About what?" Sean responded, as he inspected the top of the metallic container and took a drink.

"About all of this," Rob continued, with a devilish smile. "The money, the sex, the power? All of it."

"I think," Sean replied, with a long pause, "that I could get accustomed to this."

Rob laughed heartily as he put his arm around Sean and hugged him. Sean smiled, took another quick swig from the flask, and handed it back to Rob.

"What are you two laughing about," asked Ping with a smile, who was slouching comfortably in his seat as Elena slowly caressed his thigh.

"The possibilities," Rob said proudly, as he continued to laugh. "The possibilities."

Twenty-One

Avery stood alone in front of the bathroom mirror, wiping her nose with a Kleenex that she pulled from her purse. She tugged on her black cocktail dress, which fit her stocky frame rather snugly. She grabbed both of her breasts from outside her dress and pushed them up forcibly, helping to create a bit more cleavage. She threw her tissue away, opened her purse, and applied a fresh coat of lipstick before rinsing her hands off in the sink. As she turned to leave, she was approached by a woman who had just left one of the stalls and had scurried up behind her.

"I'm so embarrassed," confessed the woman, who had long, straight blonde hair and was wearing a pair of large sunglasses and gray business suit. "Can you help me?"

"Sure, what's wrong?" Avery asked.

"Well, you're with Anjelica's group, right?" asked the woman as Avery nodded. "I thought I saw you on the bus. You are so pretty."

"Thank you," gushed Avery, as she smiled and rolled her eyes.

"Well, I'm with her group too, and I've lost my phone," the woman continued. "I've been looking everywhere but I can't find it."

"That's terrible," Avery said with concern.

"I know," said the woman, as her voice crackled with desperation, "and the worst part is that I need to get online right now and check my payment information."

"You can use mine," Avery volunteered, as she pulled her cell phone out of her purse and handed it to the woman.

"Oh, thank you," said the woman, as she took the phone from Avery. "You are such a lifesaver."

"It's nothing, really," Avery said. "I'm headed back to our seats if you just want to bring it down to me when you're finished."

"That would be great, thank you again," said the woman as she leaned in and hugged Avery. "Oh, and one more thing - could you please keep this a secret? You know, between just us girls? If Anjelica found out that I lost my phone and had to borrow someone else's then I'd never hear the end of it."

"I promise," replied Avery, as she smiled and turned toward the doorway of the restroom. "I don't want you to get in trouble. It'll be our little secret."

Sean sat quietly in his seat as the horses that were competing in the first race slowly walked out onto the track towards the starting gate. Suddenly, Avery appeared, holding a pair of plastic cups. After maneuvering through the row, she handed Sean a cup and sat down next to him.

"That took a little while," Sean remarked. "Is everything okay?"

"It couldn't be better," beamed Avery, as she took a sip of her drink. "I made a new girlfriend."

"Oh, really?" asked Sean, as he smiled and took a drink of his bourbon.

"But that's all I can tell you," added Avery, in a playful, childlike tone.

"Okay," responded Sean slowly, sporting a confused look on his face. "Well, your timing is perfect - you're just in time for the first race."

"Marvelous!" replied Avery, as she took another sip of her drink. "Can we place a bet? Can we, Sean?"

"Sure," Sean said, as he pointed towards the horses that were slowly parading before them on the track. "Is there one of them out there that you like?"

"The one wearing the blue blanket!" shrieked Avery, which drew laughs from nearly everyone in the row.

"Those are called 'silks', Avery," Rob interjected, as he smiled and shook his head.

"Okay," Sean said, as he patted her leg. "Do you think he'll win, place or show?"

Avery seemed confused by the question, as she wrinkled her nose and turned her head sideways.

"Do you think he'll come in first, second, or third?" asked Rob, while still sporting a grin.

"First!" responded Avery enthusiastically, as she raised her arms in a triumphant gesture. "How much should we bet? Is $100 appropriate?"

"That's a perfect amount," Sean replied, smiling at both Avery and Rob.

"$100 to win!" Avery shouted, as she reached into her purse and pulled out a $100 bill and gave it to Sean.

"You better hurry, Sean," added Colby, "they're going off in about 5 minutes."

"Okay, got it," Sean said, as he stood up from his seat and began making his way through the row. "I'll be right back."

Sean glided up the steps and entered the mezzanine, where he quickly found a betting window with a relatively short line of people gathered in front of it. As he looked at the television screen that was mounted on the ceiling near the window, he suddenly found himself in front of the window.

"$100 on #6 to win," Sean said, as he handed the bill to the female track employee and placed his drink on the counter. She nodded at Sean, and then printed out a small, white ticket, handed it to him and thanked him. As Sean picked up his drink and began to leave the window, he heard a voice coming from a man who was standing in line behind him.

"That looks like a good bet," said Detective Wyatt, who was draped in the same gray trench coat that Sean saw him wearing at the airport. "I hope you win a lot of money."

"Detective Wyatt," Sean responded, with a look of surprise in his eyes. "I didn't expect to run into you here."

"Life is full of surprises now, isn't it, Sean?" Wyatt replied. "Do you have a few minutes? There's something that we need to talk about."

"Actually, now's not a good time," Sean said, as he began walking away from the betting window and across the concrete floor towards the stairway. "I'm here with some people and they're expecting me."

"Well, you wouldn't want to keep Anjelica Reardon waiting," Wyatt retorted, "or the woman with whom you're being paid to have sex."

Sean stopped dead in his tracks. He felt sick in his stomach, and a chill ran over his body. He took a quick breath, trying his best to mask his uneasiness as he turned around to face Wyatt.

"What are you talking about?" Sean asked, with a puzzled look on his face.

"Now do you have a few minutes?" Wyatt asked, as he motioned to a group of patio tables that was nearby. Sean walked over to the tables, finding a vacant one that sat by itself and overlooked the track. He drew another breath, and placed his drink on the tall, white metal table as Wyatt followed a few steps behind him.

"I still don't know what you're talking about," said Sean, as he stood awkwardly next to the table.

"It's over, Sean," replied Wyatt with an arrogant smirk.

"What's over?" Sean asked, with a quiet calm that he did his best to muster.

"I know," Wyatt replied, placing his forearm on the table as he leaned closer to Sean. "I know about Anjelica, I know that she's running an escort service, and I know that you're one of her gigolos."

"That's crazy," Sean said as he felt himself beginning to perspire beneath his shirt. "She owns a transportation business and I'm one of her drivers - nothing more."

"Is that so?" asked Wyatt gruffly, as he listened carefully to Sean.

"Look at me," Sean continued, as he lowered his voice and leaned closer to the detective. "Do I look like a gigolo? Do you actually think that women would pay to have sex with me? I'm a normal guy with a normal job, that's all."

"Methinks thou doth protest too much," replied Wyatt, with a cocky smirk on his face.

"What?" asked Sean, with genuine surprise.

"It's Shakespeare," answered Wyatt, as he shrugged and rolled his eyes. "Hamlet, Act 2, Scene 3. You can stand there and deny it all you want to, but I know that you're guilty, Sean. You lost your job, your wife, your money - then you had to make ends meet. The trouble is that what you're doing is against the law."

The crowd erupted as the horses fired out of the starting gate, causing the crowd to stir with hopeful excitement. Their gleeful shouts and screams filled the grandstand and spilled into the mezzanine where Sean and Wyatt were standing. Sean looked silently at Wyatt as the noise echoed throughout the open room. As Sean looked at the officer, he found himself overcome by a different set of feelings. He was both angry and confident, which surprised him considering that Wyatt was right about everything he was saying. This angered Sean, who suddenly felt a primal urge to protect what was his - his money, his status, and now, most importantly, his freedom. He also felt a resurgence of confidence flowing through this blood

- the same confidence that was rekindled when he began his new profession - a profession in which women paid for the privilege of his company, as well as his body. Before, this confidence was steadily growing, much like a rising tide in the ocean. Now, as he had come face-to-face with the man who wanted to take away everything he had worked for, it swept over him like a tidal wave.

"Okay, I get it," Wyatt continued, as he peered over the wall and watched the horses gallop around the track. "You're not going to say anything - and that's fine. But if you decide to talk, there might be something in it for you - a deal, of sorts. But if you decide that silence is your better option, rest assured that you'll go down with Anjelica, and you'll go down hard. Your face will be all over the TV, the newspapers, social media - you name it. Your reputation will be shot - you'll never get a good job in this town again."

Wyatt looked back at Sean, grasping the edge of the table firmly with both of his hands and he stared coldly into his eyes.

"Worst of all," Wyatt said slowly and deliberately, with icy candor, "would be the shame that you brought your family. Your parents - the people who raised you and sacrificed for you - watching as you disgraced not only yourself, but them as well? Or how about your ex-wife? Sure, you may not be married to her anymore, but she's still the mother of your child. Are you willing to put her through all of that? And speaking of your son - his name is Braden, isn't it - Could you imagine how Braden will feel when he watches his own father being arrested right before his eyes?"

Sean gritted his teeth and returned Wyatt's icy stare with one of his own.

"I'll go now," Wyatt said, as he pulled a pair of sunglasses from the inside pocket of his coat and placed them over his eyes. "I'm sure that you still have my card. Call me when you're ready to talk."

"The lady doth protest too much, methinks," replied Sean, from behind his angry expression.

"What?" responded Wyatt, as he slipped his hands into his pockets.

"You screwed up the quote. It's 'the lady doth protest too much, methinks'," continued Sean, with a venomous tone to his voice. And it's not Act 2, Scene 3 - it's Act 3, Scene 2. It's what Hamlet tells Gertrude when he thinks she's lying to him."

"Gertrude was lying to him," responded Wyatt with a smile. "Just like you're lying to me now, Sean."

"Methinks you can kiss my ass," Sean said, as he took his drink, turned, and walked down the stairway.

Wyatt smiled and began making his way toward the exit. As he strode confidently through the breezeway, the crowd erupted in cheers as the horses crossed the finish line. Wyatt wormed his way between the cars in the parking lot until he found his own. He clicked the button on his keys, which unlocked the doors and emitted a slight chirp. As he opened his door and sat down behind the steering wheel, he looked over to see a blonde woman in a gray suit sitting in the passenger seat next to him.

"Jackpot," she said, as she proudly held up a cell phone in front of Wyatt's face as he started the engine of his car.

"So I take it things went smoothly?" Wyatt asked, as he drove slowly through the grass and made his way onto a gravel driveway.

"Very," said the woman, as she removed the blonde wig from her head, tossing it in the backseat. It was Abby, who flipped down the passenger visor and began fixing her long, red hair back into place after gently placing the phone back in her lap.

"Have you had a chance to look at it yet?" Wyatt inquired, as he slowly pulled up to a stoplight and flipped on his turn signal.

"I have, and it's incredible," replied Abby, as she flipped back the visor and began swiping her finger across the screen. "The poor girl doesn't have a security code, so getting in was easy. Now here's the best part - I thought that I'd have to dig through her call history, look through her texts - which I'll still have to do, mind you - but I found something even better."

"Well, don't keep me in suspense," Wyatt responded flippantly. "I'm an old man, remember. I can die anytime."

"Ha ha," Abby said sarcastically. "There's actually an app on her phone that tells us just about everything we need to know."

"An app?" Wyatt asked, as he pulled slowly onto the main thoroughfare.

"Yep," Abby replied, as she touched the screen again, this time more forcefully, with her forefinger. "They apparently call it 'Blue Shirts' - makes sense because every time I see a guy that works for Anjelica he's decked out in a blue shirt."

"Blue Shirts?" Wyatt responded, as he furrowed his brow. "Sounds kind of boring. You'd think that she could come up with a better name than that."

"Well, it needs to be inconspicuous," added Abby. "What do you expect her to call it, Rent-a-Dick?"

"That has a certain ring to it," said Wyatt smugly.

"Anyhow, the app doesn't mention anything sexual of course," Abby continued. "It's set up to look like a limousine service or something. But the prices these women are paying to be 'chauffeured' are ridiculous. There's a 3-day package deal on here for $10,000. Can you believe it? $10,000 for a driver? Driver, my ass - nobody spends that kind of money for that, and I don't care how rich you are."

"I could get a boat for that kind of money," Wyatt mumbled. "A really nice boat."

"So did you talk to Everett?" Abby asked, as he continued to look through Avery's cell phone.

"I did," answered Wyatt. "I think it went pretty well. I told him what we knew, and that if he was willing to play ball that we might be willing to help him out."

"Do you think he's a team player?" Abby responded, and she looked up from the phone and over toward Wyatt. "Do you think he'll roll over on Anjelica to save his own ass?"

"We'll see," Wyatt said, as his thoughts drifted back to the confrontation with Sean that happened only moments ago.

"So how close are we to moving in on this?" Abby inquired, as she placed the phone in her purse. "We've got just about everything we need, don't we?"

"Almost," replied Wyatt, as he adjusted his sunglasses and checked his rearview mirror. "The biggest thing that we're lacking is probable cause. Sure, you and I know what Anjelica Reardon is doing, but a judge is going to need to a lot more to go on than just our word."

"But what about Luzzato?" pleaded Abby. "Or the information on this cell phone? It pretty much spells it out in black and white."

"The girl's phone might end up being useful," Wyatt continued, "but unless you can find somewhere in the app or in her texts that she's paying for sex, then it might not be of help after all. And as for Luzzato, I'd rather not deal with him if I can help it. His testimony might help us but it's not guaranteed. A deal with him puts him back on the streets, and that's something that I'd like to avoid if possible."

"Unless Everett talks," Abby added, as she tilted her head and began examining their options. "He spills the beans on Anjelica and her operation, then we can arrest her and every Blue Shirt we can get our hands on. The convictions start piling up, thanks to Everett's testimony. Luzzato stays in jail, Everett gets to walk, and you and I become legends in the department for bringing down the 'best little whorehouse in the Bluegrass'."

"Not everybody wins," observed Wyatt, as he glanced over at Abby and smiled. "Everett wouldn't do any time, but his punishment would be much worse than prison - because everyone would know what he did. Whether he signs an affidavit or testifies on the stand, it's still public record. The world would find out that he was a prostitute, and the press will have a field day with it. He might get a few pats on the back from his buddies, but he's guaranteed to lose the respect of everyone around him, especially those who he cared about the most. That's a sting that will hurt him the rest of his life."

"Makes sense," Abby agreed. "We're still talking about misdemeanors here, right? We could round up every gigolo in the place and they're still going to bail out the next morning. The only one that stands to do any time is Anjelica because she's running the place, right?"

"That's true, for the most part," Wyatt replied. "If the men that work for her have relatively clean criminal histories, it's doubtful that they'll do any time. Maybe a fine, a slap on the wrist, and then they'll go their merry way. Same goes for the women who are "procuring their wares", so to speak. If they can afford $10,000 a weekend for one of those clowns, they can definitely afford lawyers who can make all of this go away in a hurry. But with Anjelica, it's an entirely different story. She'll be charged with pimping and pandering, both of which are felonies. She'd be looking at some serious jail time and a few other headaches along the way."

"Like what?" asked Abby.

"Tax headaches," replied Wyatt. "In most of these cases, a lot of money is changing hands and nobody is paying taxes on that money. It doesn't matter how you make it - whether it's legally or illegally - you have to give Uncle Sam his cut or you're guilty of tax evasion. If we can find her financial records - whether she keeps them on a computer, or some type of ledger - that would go a long way in helping to seal the deal. Even if she and her men are paying taxes on their ill-gotten gains, we would still have another key piece of evidence to help us prove that she's running an escort service."

"What if Everett doesn't cooperate?" Abby asked, as she crossed her legs and pulled her sunglasses out of her purse. "I could go undercover - I could pose as a client and use the girl's phone to set up a date with one of the man whores. We could set up a sting operation right there at the house. I could wear a wire, talk business with the guy - then you could bust in the door and take everybody down - end of story."

"Out of the question," Wyatt responded, shaking his head in disapproval.

"Why not?" replied Abby, as she put on her sunglasses.

"If the girl's in the house she might recognize you," countered Wyatt. "It's too big of a risk. She's also likely to tell someone about her phone, in which case that house will be on lockdown and everyone will be on red alert."

"So we wait it out for a little while?" Abby asked with a groan.

"Precisely," answered Wyatt, "and right now you and I are the only ones at the department that know about this. I'd like to keep it that way for the time being. We would need someone else at the department to sign off on a sting, and I don't want to go down that road just yet."

"Everett will crack," Abby said confidently. "The guy's a pencil pusher and family man - probably coaches his son's soccer team for all we know. He's likely just a nice guy that got caught up in something that he shouldn't have. I seriously doubt that he'll drag this thing out. He's got too much to lose."

"That's what I'm banking on," Wyatt remarked solemnly.

Back at Keeneland, the last race was moments away from beginning, and Sean found himself stewing silently in his seat as the horses neared the starting gate. The weather had cooled considerably, and most of the guests in Anjelica's group were now donning jackets, coats, gloves and scarves. Avery, who had imbibed a bit too much bourbon throughout the day, had fallen asleep in her seat, and her head was resting comfortably on Sean's shoulder. Just past her on his left he saw Rob and Colby engaged in a deep conversation with Patricia and Diane, who had huddled together in their seats, rubbing their hands occasionally to generate warmth. Before he knew it, the race had ended and Anjelica began leading her guests out of their seats and up the aisle. Sean pulled Avery gently from her seat, which woke her and brought a smile to her face as she stumbled against him. He looked up to see Rob, who was now standing next to Avery as well, extending his arm as well so he could help her to her feet. Rob smiled at Sean as both men led her past the seats and into the aisle.

"Where are we going?" she slurred, as Sean placed his arm under her shoulders. "Is it over? Don't tell me it's over."

"It's over," Sean replied softly, as he walked her up the stairway.

Twenty-Two

It was now 4 a.m., and Sean was lying in bed next to Avery. With his hands tucked tightly behind his head, he stared at the ceiling, unable to sleep. He tried to close his eyes, but Avery's snoring was too much of a distraction. She had slept most of the evening, having passed out just after the bus returned to Anjelica's house after the outing at the race track. After carrying her upstairs, Sean had helped her into her pajamas and put her in the bed. She had managed to sleep through the party downstairs as the guests frolicked in the living room below - dancing, drinking, and enthusiastically reminiscing on the day's events.

As he turned away from Avery, he looked through the shadows of the room at his blue dress shirt, which was dangling from a hanger on the doorknob of the closet. As he stared at the shirt, he couldn't stop thinking about his conversation with Detective Wyatt earlier that afternoon. Although he was rattled by the exchange with the officer, who seemed to take far too much delight in the fact that he was on the precipice of toppling Anjelica's organization, Sean also felt angry. He was angry at himself for joining Blue Shirts, knowing that there was always a chance that a day would come and his secret would be discovered. At first, the thought of being arrested was just that - a thought - but now it had become a reality. Wyatt knew too much, and it seemed certain that it would be a matter of days before the detective took action against the company, Anjelica, and himself. Sean crawled out of bed, walked down the hallway, and slowly turned the doorknob of the guest room that he saw Rob enter earlier in the evening.

"We need to talk," Sean said to Rob, as he entered the darkened room and saw his friend sprawled out in bed next to Patricia, who was fast asleep and buried under several layers of covers.

"Sean, is that you?" mumbled Rob, as he slowly opened his eyes to see his friend standing beside the bed.

"Yeah, it's me," Sean whispered. "Can you meet me downstairs?"

"Can't this wait until morning?" answered Rob, as he closed his eyes and nudged his head into his pillow.

"It is morning," Sean replied, "so get up."

"This better be important," Rob groaned, as he slid out from underneath the covers and followed Sean downstairs.

As the early morning sun began peeking through the first floor windows, Sean and Rob made their way through the living room and into the kitchen. It was very quiet, as all of the other guests were still asleep throughout the house. Rob flipped on the light and started the coffee maker, as he continued to sleepily rub his eyes.

"So what's this about?" Rob asked, as he folded his arms and leaned back against the counter.

"It's about the police," Sean replied, as Rob looked on with confusion. "One of them stopped me yesterday at the racetrack. He said he knows about Anjelica, knows about the whole operation, knows about me."

"You're kidding, right?" Rob replied, as he furrowed his brow.

"I wish I was," Sean continued, with a worried look on his face.

"Who was this guy?" Rob asked, as he took a glazed doughnut off a nearby tray and inspected it. "Was he local?"

"I think so," Sean replied. "His name is Wyatt. He didn't go into a lot of specifics, but he was very confident about the way he approached me. He also made it clear that if I was willing to help him out he'd offer me a deal."

"You didn't tell him anything, did you Sean?" asked Rob, as he quickly put down his doughnut, crossed his arms and stared at his friend.

"Of course not," Sean responded, surprised at his friend's question.

"Good," Rob replied with a look of relief. "If he offered you a deal, then he probably doesn't have anything on us. He's just fishing."

"I don't know," replied Sean carefully. "I'm thinking that maybe we should at least talk about this. You know - so we can have all of the options in front of us and think about what the best plan of action would be."

"There's nothing to talk about," replied Rob angrily. "You're safe. We're safe. Just deny, deny, deny. They don't have shit on us because Anjelica has created a foolproof system. Nobody can prove that we're doing anything illegal here because we follow the letter of the law. Clients pay her, she pays us, and it's out there on Paypal for all the world to see. Don't you see? She's untouchable. We're untouchable."

"That's easy for you to say," Sean countered, "you don't have as much to lose as I do. I have a family."

"Blue Shirts is my family!" shouted Rob, as his booming voice rattled the empty wine glasses that lined the kitchen counter. "Anjelica is my family. You're my family. Don't you see? I have just as much to lose as you do."

The room suddenly became quiet, as Rob gathered himself and leaned backward against the counter. He took a deep breath, and shook his head, and stared at the floor. Sean looked at Rob, realizing at that moment just how important all of this was to him. For Sean, Blue Shirts was a way to make a living, but for Rob it was living. He had been immersed in this way of life for so long that it had consumed him. It was the reason he woke up in the morning - his only bright spot in an otherwise empty existence. It was everything to Rob, and desperation was coming over him at the thought of losing the life he had not only grown to know, but grown to love.

"If I wanted out," Sean said quietly. "What's the exit strategy? What would

I need to do?"

"Exit strategy?" Rob replied calmly, although he was still clearly agitated. "What do you mean?"

"If I left Blue Shirts," Sean answered. "What if I decided that all of this was just too much for me and I wanted to go back to my old life? How would that work?"

"You don't get it, do you?" Rob asked, as he walked across the floor and moved closer to Sean. "Nobody leaves Blue Shirts. There's no 'exit strategy', because it doesn't exist. And besides, what would you go back to? You don't have your job, you don't have your wife. You've got nothing. Do you hear me? Nothing."

Just then, Anjelica entered the kitchen, dressed in a pink cloth robe that covered her white silk pajamas.

"What the hell is going on down here?" she asked, as she alternated her angry stare at both of the men. "I could hear you upstairs in my room."

"Sean has something he wants to tell you," Rob replied.

It was now Monday afternoon, and Detective Wyatt stood stone-faced in the bedroom of a rustic house on the east side of Lexington. He stepped aside as a pair of homicide detectives with the police department began looking for evidence throughout the room. He watched as one of them examined the beige carpet that was stretched thinly across the floor. Moments later, he observed the other officer collecting the prescription pill bottles that were sitting atop the nightstand, carefully placing them in a clear, Ziploc bag. Wyatt then watched as two large paramedics pulled the lifeless body of Dr. Luzzato off the bed, and placed it on a nearby gurney. As one of the paramedics pulled a white sheet over Dr. Luzzato, Wyatt took one last look at his corpse before it was carted away to the ambulance that was waiting outside. He studied the thin red horizontal line that ran across the doctor's neck, as well as the thicker line that ran across his chest.

"Looks like an overdose," said Sergeant Blackburn, after plucking a syringe off the nightstand with a large pair of tweezers and examining it in the sunlight beaming through the window. "I knew this bastard would find some way of avoiding his trial. At least it'll save the taxpayers some money."

"Did you see the marks on his neck and his chest?" asked Wyatt. "They look like rope burns - like he might have been tied down, or restrained in some way."

"You're not homicide anymore, remember?" Blackburn coyly replied. "Besides, the coroner will be here any minute - we'll let him sort it all out."

Detective Wyatt turned away from Blackburn, exited the bedroom and walked through the empty hallway towards the front door. As he began to leave the house, he turned and walked towards the kitchen. He approached a glass patio door, slid it open, and walked outside onto a wooden deck that was overlooking an empty swimming pool in the backyard. He placed his arms on the railing of the deck and looked down at the pool. He saw the small puddles of dirty water that were sprinkled around its bottom, as well as a healthy collection of dead leaves that were clinging together near its drain. As he turned to go back inside, his cell phone rang.

"This is Wyatt," he said, answering his phone as he glanced inside through the patio door at the detectives, watching them wander into the kitchen.

"I've been thinking about your offer," said Sean, in a calm voice, which took Wyatt slightly off guard.

"And?" responded Wyatt, as he saw Sergeant Blackburn walking through the kitchen and coming towards the patio door.

"I'll help you," Sean replied, after a slight pause.

"That's a good decision, Sean," Wyatt said, as he waved at Blackburn and motioned for him to meet him in the front yard. "Where are you right now? I can meet you and you can fill out a statement - it won't take that long."

"I'm not filling out a statement," countered Sean rather quickly.

"I need a statement from you to get the ball rolling on this," Wyatt replied, as he turned his back to the door and walked across the redwood deck. "It'll take just a few minutes. Where are you? I can come to you right now."

"I can give you something better than a statement," Sean answered, "that is, if you're interested."

"I'm listening," Wyatt responded curiously.

"She has a book that she keeps in her house," continued Sean. "She keeps it locked in a safe that's behind a painting in her living room. The book has everything that you would want, including all of the company's financial information and her client list."

"Do you have access to the book?" asked Wyatt, as he paced excitedly across the deck. "Can you bring it to me?"

"I don't want her to know that I've talked to you," Sean responded. "She's a very dangerous woman, and if she found out that I gave you the book, she would try to hurt me or my family. I can't let that happen."

"I'll just get a search warrant, go in her house, and take it myself," Wyatt remarked.

"That's actually what I was thinking," agreed Sean. "That way she won't find out that I had anything to do with you getting the book. It's always in the safe, so you can come in and get it whenever you like. But I need to ask you something. I need to ask you for a favor, if that's all right."

"A favor?" asked Wyatt in a condescending tone. "And what would that be?"

"This coming weekend is her busiest of the year, and she's celebrating it by having a huge party this Saturday night," replied Sean. "Her house is going to be filled with her biggest clients and most all of her employees. Showing up then would be the ultimate embarrassment. She and her guests don't deserve to be raided - that would be too humiliating for everyone inside the house. Just use discretion, and more importantly, please don't do it this Saturday night."

"I can't make any promises," responded Wyatt, as he made his way down the steps of the deck and around the side of the house.

"I understand," Sean replied, as his voice trailed off quietly.

A few minutes later, Wyatt walked into the precinct and saw Abby standing over her desk, placing a few pieces of paper on a stack of folders. As she finished organizing the papers, she glanced one last time at the clock on the wall and retrieved a set of car keys from her purse. Wyatt walked in, sporting a large smile, and he plopped down on the corner of her desk without saying a word.

"I take it that you've heard about Luzzato?" Abby asked.

Wyatt nodded and continued to stare off in the distance.

"Then what are you so happy about?" she asked, as she dropped the rest of the papers she was holding down onto her desk. "He was the key to this whole Anjelica Reardon case."

"He was the key," Wyatt replied. "I just got off the phone with Everett. He's gonna play ball."

"I can't believe it - that's amazing!" Abby responded loudly enough to draw glances from some of the other officers in the room. "You got them."

"We got them," Wyatt said as he turned toward his partner. "There's no way I could have done this without you. You're a hell of a cop."

"And we make a hell of a team," replied Abby, as she smiled at Wyatt. "So how's all of this going down, Detective? Is Everett coming in to give us a statement?"

"He's not coming to us," answered Wyatt. "We're going to him."

"A sting?" Abby asked excitedly. "Does that mean I get to buy a new wig?"

"You can save your money," replied Wyatt with a smile. "Everett verified the existence of Anjelica Reardon's client book. She keeps it in a safe in her living room, and it's got everything in there that we need to take down her whole operation - client lists, transaction information, the money trail - everything."

"Is he just going to give it to us?" Abby inquired with a bewildered look on her face.

"Not exactly," Wyatt answered. "Everett doesn't want Anjelica or the rest of her crew to know that he rolled over on them, so I'm going to write a search warrant for the book and go to her house and take it."

"Is Everett expecting something in return?" Abby asked.

"He didn't ask for a deal, and even if he did I wouldn't give him one," replied Wyatt. "He's just as guilty as Anjelica Reardon or any of the other people who are involved in her business."

"He's probably been looking for a way out anyway," added Abby. "He's only been working for them for a few weeks, and I seriously doubt that he has any desire to go down with the ship. Anjelica has the most to lose here and Everett knows that. He's likely thinking that she'll get all of the publicity and jail time, and that he and the other Blue Shirts will get a slap on the wrist. The sad thing is that he's probably right."

"It might not be that easy for him, especially if it goes to trial." Wyatt responded. "Everett would likely be called to testify and things would get messy. Anjelica would find out that he told us where the book was, which would put his life in danger."

"Danger?" asked Abby.

"What happened to Luzzato probably wasn't an overdose," continued Wyatt. "He knew way too much about Blue Shirts, and I'm sure that Anjelica Reardon had caught wind of the fact that he would soon be sharing with us everything that he knew. My guess is that she had something to do with his death."

"That may very well be true," Abby replied, "but you know as well as I do that Everett and the other Blue Shirts aren't going to trial. They're going to plead out, and all of Anjelica's clients will do the same. They'll all want to avoid the publicity. The only way any of them will have to testify is if Anjelica wants to fight this and go to trial. This seems unlikely since it would bring a lot of negative attention not only to herself, but also to all of her high-profile clients. Everett probably figures that his part in all of this will be viewed as relatively minor, so long as he keeps a low profile."

"We might not be able to bring him to court," Wyatt responded with a savvy glint in his eye, "but who says we can't bring the court to him?"

"I'm not sure that I follow," asked Abby, puzzled by Wyatt's cryptic comment.

"The court of public opinion," Wyatt continued, as he leaned forward and stood up next to Abby. "When we show up at Anjelica's house, we won't be alone. We're going to have the media there with us - the newspaper and all the local TV stations. You and I will go into the house, get the book, and then when we come back out, I'll give a little speech to the camera crews to let them know that we've just taken down the biggest prostitution ring that the city has seen since the 19th century."

"Reporters, news vans, lights, cameras," Abby added, "it's going to be a media circus. Are you sure that's a good idea?"

"It's a great idea," replied Wyatt. "Like you said, most of them aren't going to be punished, so we'll let the media take care of that for us. Once we have the book, we'll take it back to the station to examine its contents and proceed accordingly. Meanwhile, the TV crews will camp out on Anjelica's lawn until she, Everett, and the rest of the bunch decide to come out."

"A 'walk of shame' so to speak?" Abby said with a smirk. "How oddly appropriate. So when is this going to take place?"

"This Saturday night," Wyatt responded sharply. "Anjelica is having a big shindig at her house that evening. Everett says that the entire staff has been put on notice that they have to be there because she's expecting most of her VIP clients to attend."

"Are we making any arrests or are we just retrieving the book?" Abby asked, as she circled the desk.

"Right now we don't have anything concrete on them," Wyatt replied, "so we're not making any arrests at this point. That will likely change after we process the book of course. We'll see who's in it, examine their financial activity with the company, and proceed from there."

"It sounds easy enough," Abby said with a slight hesitation, "but aren't you worried?"

"About what?" replied Wyatt, shrugging a bit as he answered her question.

"You know the old expression about how you shouldn't put all of your eggs in one basket?" Abby continued. "It's not Shakespeare but I'm sure that you've heard it before."

"I'm familiar with it, why do you ask?" Wyatt responded.

"Well, at the moment that book is the only piece of evidence that we have, and we don't even have it yet," replied Abby. "Sure, I have that girl's cell phone, but the method in which I acquired it wasn't exactly by the book."

"You mean when you stole that phone?" said Wyatt sarcastically.

"'Stole' is such a harsh word," Abby countered with a smile. "I prefer 'liberated'. Regardless, with Luzzato out of the picture and no statement from Everett, everything that we have in this case hinges on that book. If we hold off on that for now we could do some more surveillance, set up a sting, and bring some of the men in her organization in for questioning, it will definitely strengthen our case. We would eventually get our hands on that book too."

"I see what you're saying," Wyatt replied defiantly, "but we might not get this chance again. The longer we wait - the more of a chance that Everett will tip off Anjelica. If that happens, you know as well as I do that they could all disappear. If they find out that we're onto them then it changes everything, and it will make our ob almost impossible. It's best to strike now when they're least expecting it. This way we have the element of surprise on our side."

"You're not fooling me, Tom," Abby responded. "I know you. I know that, to you, this case is still all about Everett. And I know that going through with that plan of yours is all about Everett too. I know exactly how Saturday night will play out. We'll go in, the party will come to a screeching halt, and everyone in the room will start pointing fingers at each other wondering who told the police about the book. With Everett being the new guy, Anjelica and the rest of the Blue Shirts will probably think that he tipped us off, which will no doubt make his life there a living hell. But his real nightmare will come when he, like all of her other male escorts, comes out of the house to face the media that's going to be camped out on the front lawn hoping to land interviews with everyone who'll be trying to slink out of that house undetected. Whether it's that night, the next day, or whenever - the news crews will eventually see him leave, he'll eventually be identified, and his name and face will then be all over the news. His life as he knows it will be over, and you'll win. Then all of this will be over, right Tom?"

"It's going to be over one way or the other," Wyatt replied after a long pause, "and I'm going in this weekend with or without you. It's your choice."

"I'll be there," Abby responded. "I just hope that book is there too."

Twenty-Three

It was now Saturday evening, and Anjelica's house was brimming with activity. One by one, the gentlemen of Blue Shirts arrived at the front door, each of them clad in black tuxedos, white shirts, and black bowties. Each man was accompanied by a female client, all of whom looked stunning - as if they were walking the red carpet of a Hollywood movie premiere. Dressed in expensive, designer gowns and wearing decadent amounts of jewelry, the women entered the foyer and were immediately greeted by both Anjelica and Samson. Anjelica, who was wearing a sequined gray dress that hugged her athletic figure, gushed over how beautiful each woman looked, showering each of them with an array of compliments, kisses and lingering hugs. As Samson took each woman's coat, he too would kiss them, as well as flirt with them, as they filtered through the hallway and into the living room.

Rob entered the home holding hands with Patricia, the woman he had taken to the race track the previous weekend. Patricia grinned at Samson, and handed Rob her coat. Rob then immediately handed it to Samson.

"Every time she smiles I keep expecting her face to crack," Samson whispered to Rob.

"You and me both," Rob whispered back to Samson before discreetly turning away, taking Patricia's hand, and leading her out of the room.

Next was Colby, sporting a black cowboy hat with his tuxedo, along with Diane, who had been his date from the previous weekend.

"So good to see you again," Anjelica beamed. "Are you having a good time with Colby?"

"Oh, girl, he's sweeter than apple butter," Diane replied in her sharp, country twang. "Back in Texas it's hard to find a gentleman like him. I think I'm gonna have to pack him up and take him back there with me when I leave Kentucky."

"Well, it's alright with me if it's alright with Colby," said Anjelica jokingly as she looked at Colby. "You don't mind, do you Colby?"

"No, not a bit," responded Colby with a chuckle. "As a matter of fact, I'd fit right in down there."

"How's that?" asked Anjelica, trying to stifle her laughter.

"Well, you know what they say," Colby remarked. "Everything's bigger in Texas."

"Oh, you're awful," Diane squealed as she playfully slapped Colby's chest. As the pair made their way through the hallway, Ping was the next to arrive. He was holding the hand of a short, elderly lady who looked to be in her eighties. The woman, who was wearing a mink stole, a fur hat, and a black, glittery dress, moved slowly into the foyer where she was greeted by Anjelica.

"Lillian, so good to see you again!" exclaimed Anjelica, as she embraced the older woman. "How have you been?"

"Oh, I can't complain," answered the woman, in a low, husky baritone. "Any day above ground is a good day I suppose."

"Very much so," Anjelica agreed, as she took Lillian's hand and led her into the living room.
Colby then slid over next to Ping and put his arm around his shoulder.

"You're gonna be earning every penny this weekend," said Colby, with a wry smile. "Did you hear that? Every penny."

"Screw you," replied Ping, as he scowled at Colby and then walked downtrodden into the living room.

Upstairs in Avery's bedroom, Sean was staring at his reflection in the mirror as he fumbled with his bowtie. He tried repeatedly to tie it, but each attempt proved unsuccessful. Frustrated, he pulled the tie off and threw it on the dresser.

"What's wrong?" Avery asked, rising from the bed and coming over to Sean. "You've been tense all night. Is everything okay?"

"I'm fine," Sean replied curtly as he glanced back and forth at the floor and the mirror. Avery moved closer to him.

"You don't seem fine," she said as she put her hands on his shoulders. "Let me help."

Avery took the black bowtie from the dresser and placed it around Sean's neck. As she slipped her fingers under his collar, his eyes continued to dart nervously around the room. His breathing was heavier than normal, and he was hoping that Avery wouldn't notice it as her arms rested firmly against his chest. He looked into Avery's large, brown eyes, which were fixated on Sean's shirt collar, and felt the urge to tell her why he had been acting so strangely tonight. But he knew that he couldn't.

"There," Avery said. "All done."

"Wow, I'm impressed," Sean said as he turned toward the mirror and looked at the bowtie, which was tied perfectly around his collar. "You're a woman of many talents."

"Not really," Avery replied, "but I watched you over the last hour struggling with it and thought that I might give it a try. I guess it was just beginner's luck."

"Beginner's luck, huh?" asked Sean, as he tugged lightly on the sides of the bowtie.

"I suppose so," replied Avery, as her voice softened. "I guess you could say I've been lucky my whole life. I was lucky to be born into a wealthy family, attend expensive schools, and live in a nice home. But most of all, I'm lucky that my mother sent me to live with Anjelica these last few weeks. If she hadn't, I would have never met you. You are everything I've ever wanted in my life, and I've felt that way from the moment that I first saw you. I love you, Sean."

Sean stood speechless in front of Avery, who now stood silently herself - waiting for him to answer. Even though he had suspected this for a while, it was still surprising to hear Avery's confession. He took a quick breath, stifling the uneasiness that had suddenly begun to set in, and he placed his hand under her chin.

"Oh, Avery," he responded compassionately, trying his best to mask the disappointment in his voice.

"I need to know," Avery continued, "and please, be honest. Do you love me too?"

Sean knew that he wasn't in love with Avery, but as he looked deeply into her eyes, he considered telling her otherwise. He wondered if he should tell her that he had feelings for her as well, reasoning that keeping her happy would be best for the company - as she was first and foremost a client, albeit indirectly through her mother. But protecting the company was the last thing on his mind right now, and he knew in his heart that it would be best to be truthful with her. Although he didn't love her, Sean had grown close to her over the last few weeks. He considered her a friend, and he reasoned that lying to her now would lead to a great deal of heartbreak later. He placed his hands on her arms and began to answer Avery's question when Rob appeared suddenly in the bedroom doorway.

"Knock, knock," Rob said, holding a bottle of champagne tucked under his arm. "Anjelica needs you both downstairs. It's almost show time."

Sean was instantly relieved, as Rob's arrival provided the perfect escape from answering Avery's question. Avery, on the other hand, was distraught. She stared at Rob for a moment, then looked back at Sean with her big, brown eyes.

"Sounds great," Sean said to Rob as he took Avery's hand and smiled. Avery petulantly rolled her eyes before Sean began walking toward Rob with her in tow. They followed Rob into the hallway, and then down the stairway.

Outside on the street, Detective Wyatt was sitting in his parked car, waiting silently in the darkness. He peered through his windshield, watching as the last of the guests entered Anjelica's home. As the front door closed for the last time, he glanced down the street at the other vehicles that were parked along the curb. He marveled at the long row of black SUVs, each one more expensive than the next, that were positioned perfectly alongside the sidewalk. Although it was very dark, he had a clear view of the house - especially the two large windows that flanked either side of the front door. He watched as the guests inside the home moved past the windows, casting long shadows across the front lawn until they eventually disappeared from view. He ran his hand across the front of his badge, which was attached to a lanyard that was wrapped around his neck and turned to Abby, who was sitting next to him in the passenger seat.

"You remember what to do?" asked Wyatt in a stern voice.

"How could I forget?" Abby replied as she rolled her eyes. "You've only gone over it a thousand times."

For the next two hours, the detectives continued to observe the house. Occasionally, they could hear a burst of laughter that would be loud enough to penetrate the walls of the house, or see a small gathering of guests passing by one of the front windows. One thing was constant though - the music, which was steadily playing throughout the night. It was muffled, but yet still unusually loud for such an older neighborhood.

"It's 10:45 p.m. and the bass is still thumping," Abby remarked as she glanced at her cell phone. "If we don't find the book, we can always cite them for violating the noise ordinance."

Wyatt smiled, and then noticed a pair of headlights pulling up behind him. He adjusted his rearview mirror then opened the door of his car.

"They're here," he said, as he and Abby exited the car and approached the large vehicle that was now parked behind them. It was a television news van, and its stark white color looked very out of place among the dark-colored vehicles that were lined up and down the darkened street. Moments later, another white van arrived, followed closely by another. Almost in unison, the vehicles parked, turned off their headlights, and then turned off their engines. From the passenger side of each van sprang a female reporter, each of whom rushed over to Wyatt and Abby.

"Detective Wyatt?" asked the first reporter, a beautiful blonde woman in her twenties who was wearing a heavy, dark blue coat. "I'm Morgan Whitlock - we spoke on the phone."

Wyatt nodded and introduced Morgan to Abby as the other reporters, along with their cameramen, quickly approached.

"So what's going on here?" Morgan asked. "It must be something big or you wouldn't have invited all of us here tonight, right?"

"It's big all right," Wyatt replied. "But that's all that I'm saying right now."

"What can you give me now?" Morgan asked. "The station has already told us that this is tonight's lead-in story on our 11 o'clock newscast. We're going 'live' here in a few minutes, so I have to tell them something."

"Here's how it's going to play out," Wyatt shared with the reporters and their cameramen, who were beginning to set up their equipment along the sidewalk. "Detective Miles and I will be entering the house that's directly behind me. Shortly thereafter, we'll come back outside and in my hands I'll be holding a key piece of evidence in a criminal investigation that will shake this city to its very foundations. At that time, I will give a statement regarding the specific nature of the investigation, and briefly answer any questions that you might have before I depart to police headquarters to deliver the evidence."

"What kind of evidence?" asked Morgan hurriedly, "What crime?"

"Your questions will be answered soon enough," replied Wyatt smugly. "I would also strongly encourage all of you to remain here throughout the night, and to keep your cameras rolling, as every person who is currently inside this house is involved in this investigation. You might be surprised to see who's connected to this case. In a few minutes we're going in, so get ready."

As the reporters returned to their news vans, Abby placed her hands on her hips and glared at Wyatt.

"'Live' TV?" she remarked aggressively. "Really? Are you sure that you want to go through with this? Just to shame a poor guy that's caught up in something that he shouldn't be?"

"The law is the law," Wyatt replied coolly, "and when you break the law, there are consequences."

"Fine," resigned Abby, with a slight shrug of her shoulders. As she turned away from Wyatt, she looked over toward Anjelica's house and noticed something peculiar.

"That's odd," she said, as she raised her hand to point at the house. "Weren't all of the lights on a minute ago?"

Wyatt turned toward the home to see that all of the interior lights had been turned off, and with the exception of the meager glow coming from the front porch light, the house was dark. It was also silent as well.

"Do you hear that?" Wyatt asked. "They've turned off the music too."

"No lights, no music," Abby added. "What the hell is going on in there?"

"We're about to find out," answered Wyatt, as he pulled a search warrant out of the pocket of his coat.

The detectives cautiously walked onto the driveway, then maneuvered onto the small sidewalk that led to the front door. It was still very quiet, and as Wyatt and Abby arrived at the front porch, the bright lights from the television cameras came on suddenly, casting shadows against the front of the house. The silence in the yard was then broken by the sound of Morgan Whitlock's voice, which seemed to echo down the street. Wyatt and Abby turned away from the door and looked back toward the street to see Morgan, as well as the other two reporters, positioned along the sidewalk. As the camera lights glared, the three reporters were beginning to report from the scene.

Wyatt rang the doorbell, and a few seconds later the door opened. It was Anjelica, whose sequined gray dress reflected almost like a mirror ball in the camera lights. She greeted the officers with a warm smile.

"Ms. Reardon, I presume?" Wyatt asked.

"Yes," answered Anjelica, slightly taken aback by the barrage of lights coming from the sidewalk.

"I'm Detective Wyatt with the Lexington Police Department," Wyatt said, as he held up his badge. "This is Detective Miles," he continued, as he nodded at Abby.

"Oh my," Anjelica responded, as she playfully placed her hands on the cheeks of her face. "And to what do I owe this honor? I do hope that my music wasn't too loud."

"I'm afraid it's much more serious than that," answered Wyatt. "We have a warrant to search the property."

"Oh dear, whatever for?" asked Anjelica.

"The safe in your living room," Wyatt replied, as he handed Anjelica a copy of the search warrant. "Or more specifically, its contents."

"I see," said Anjelica, squinting her eyes as she briefly looked at the paperwork in her hands. "Then by all means, come inside. It's much too cold to stay out here all night. And what about your friends on the sidewalk?"

"The television stations sent them, Ms. Reardon," answered Abby, as she entered the hallway of the foyer with Wyatt. "They'll be fine."

"That's nonsense," Anjelica continued. "It's freezing outside." She then loudly beckoned out to the reporters on the sidewalk. "Yoo hoo! Excuse me! Would any of you like to come inside? Have some coffee to warm you up, perhaps?"

The reporters looked at each other in confusion. Two of them then politely declined Anjelica's invitation, however Morgan considered it for a moment.

"Did she just invite us inside?" Morgan whispered to Tony, her longtime cameraman.

"Yeah," he responded. "You're not thinking about going in there, are you?"

"Of course I am," replied Morgan. "This could be the biggest story of my career. And to get it all 'live'? This is huge. Follow me."

Gripping her microphone tightly, Morgan hastily rushed through the yard toward the front porch. Tony, while packing his video camera on his right shoulder, followed closely behind. Both were out of breath as they reached Anjelica.

"I'm Morgan Whitlock," Morgan said, as she introduced herself. "I'm a reporter with WTVL."

"Oh, I recognize you now," replied Anjelica. "I'm a big fan. I'm Anjelica Reardon. Would you like to come inside for some coffee?"

"We'd love to, but we're here on a story assignment," Morgan responded, as Tony raised his camera and pointed it in Anjelica's direction. "By the way, this is Tony. Would you mind if we're recording when we're inside?"

"By all means, certainly," answered Anjelica graciously. "Film anything you like."

"Thank you, Ms. Reardon," replied Morgan, as she entered the foyer and turned around to face Tony. "Did you get that on tape?" she whispered to Tony, who nodded carefully.

A few feet away, Wyatt and Abby stood nearby in the darkness, watching as the reporter and her cameraman entered the home. They looked at each other with concern as Anjelica closed the front door. The house was very dark and quiet, and the officers listened intently to see if they could hear any noises coming from the other rooms. There was no music, and not a single voice could be heard throughout the residence, despite the fact that the detectives had seen nearly a hundred guests enter the home earlier that night.

"Is something wrong with the lights?" Wyatt asked.

"Yes, I'm dreadfully sorry," Anjelica answered. "The power just went out - it happens sometimes with an old house like this. It should come back on momentarily though."

"This should help," Tony said, as he turned the light on that was mounted to his camera. Even though it was a small light, it helped to illuminate the room.

"Oh, that's much better, thank you," said Anjelica.

"Where's your living room?" asked Wyatt purposefully.

"It's right this way, follow me," responded Anjelica, as she led everyone through the small hallway toward the back of her house.

With only the stark, bright lamp of the camera, the living room looked rather spooky. The antique furniture looked like something you would find in a haunted mansion, and paintings that adorned the walls seemed creepy as well. Most troubling to Wyatt was that there were no guests - no people visible at all - in the room. He looked nervously at Abby and contemplated reaching under his coat and into his shoulder holster to brandish his firearm.

"The safe is over there, behind my portrait of Madame Belle," said Anjelica, as she pointed toward the large piece of framed artwork that was hanging on the wall. "The safe is locked of course, but the combination is 8-11-40. That was the date she passed away. So sad."

The empty darkness of the room already had Wyatt feeling on edge, but Anjelica's helpfulness seemed very suspicious to him. He glanced at Abby, whose cautious expression confirmed that she too shared this uneasy feeling.

"Are we good?" Morgan asked Tony, who promptly gave her a thumbs up.

"We're rolling," Tony replied as he slipped a pair of headphones over his curly brown hair.

"This is Morgan Whitlock of WTVL reporting live," announced Morgan, as she clutched her microphone and stared intently into the television camera. "We're at the residence of Anjelica Reardon, whose home is on Short Street near downtown Lexington. We were summoned to the home by Detective Tom Wyatt of the Lexington Police Department, who you can see just behind me."

Tony turned his camera toward Wyatt, who by now was standing next to the portrait. He placed his hands on the side of the frame and pulled it towards him. The portrait swung open slowly, rotating on its hinges, to expose the gray safe that was hidden in the recessed compartment of the wall behind it.

"According to Detective Wyatt, the safe that he is getting ready to open contains a major piece of evidence in a criminal case that he's investigating," continued Morgan.

Wyatt looked over his shoulder at Morgan, drew a deep breath, and looked back at the safe. He noticed that the door was ajar, and he placed his hand on the bright silver latch that was beside the tumbler. As this was happening, Morgan stepped closer to Anjelica.

"With me now is Ms. Anjelica Reardon," Morgan continued. "Ms. Reardon, are you involved in the investigation, and if so, would you like to comment on it this evening?"

"It's the first I've heard of it," replied Anjelica into the microphone while smiling innocently at Morgan. Anjelica then turned towards the camera and stared seductively into its lens. "I'm just as curious as you are."

"Well there you have it," Morgan remarked, as she moved away from Anjelica and slowly made her way towards Wyatt. "Ladies and gentlemen, you are witnessing a police investigation that is in progress. We are at the home of Anjelica Reardon, a local woman who lives just a few blocks from downtown. Detective Tom Wyatt of the Lexington Police Department is just behind me, over my shoulder, and he is about to secure a piece of evidence that is relevant to the case."

Wyatt glanced nervously over his shoulder at Morgan, smiled awkwardly at the television camera, and returned his attention to the safe. He placed his hand on the tumbler, spinning it slowly and deliberately in order to ensure that the combination was correct. Once he finished, he pulled the latch handle, and the safe's silver door swung open. He peered into the small, shadowy chamber, and breathed a sigh of relief when he saw its contents - an old book with a worn, leather cover. With a confident smirk, he grabbed the book and pulled it out of the safe. He looked over at Abby, who also was smiling - albeit with relief.

"What is it?" asked Morgan to Wyatt, as she and Tony moved closer to him. "Is it a book?"

"It's much more than just a book," Wyatt replied, with renewed swagger. "It's something that will change this city forever."

"A groundbreaking discovery here at the home of Anjelica Reardon," announced Morgan, as she excitedly continued her report. "And what does the book contain?" she continued, as she turned again to face Wyatt. "Can you now share with us the details of your investigation."

Wyatt smiled again, gave Morgan a cocky nod, and opened the book. As he did, he found a pink envelope fastened snugly within the first few pages. Written on the outside of the envelope was his first name, "Tom", which he found to be quite peculiar. The envelope felt heavy in his hand, so he reached inside it, and removed a card that was inside. The card, which was light blue in color, had a handwritten note on it that read "A fool thinks himself to be wise, but a wise man knows himself to be a fool. - William Shakespeare."

A sick feeling overcame Wyatt as he hastily opened the book, only to discover that rather than it being a ledger full of client information, the pages were blank. Desperately, he leafed through the book, violently turning each page hoping to find some sort of writing or other information within it. As Wyatt raised his head, he looked at Abby, who appeared both concerned and confused. He then looked toward Morgan, who was silhouetted by the light from the camera. She was now standing in front of him eagerly waiting to hear about his discovery.

All of a sudden, the lights came on, and a deafening "Surprise!" filled the living room. As Wyatt looked around, he saw Anjelica's guests - dozens of men in tuxedoes, as well as their older, well-dressed female counterparts - standing and cheering. All of them were wearing cone-shaped party hats, blowing noise-makers, and throwing streamers across the room. Through the foyer hallway entered a pair of women holding a vast array of colorful balloons, which they released into the center of the room, bringing about more cheers from the guests. Towards the back of the room a banner was unfurled from the top of a curtain rod that read "Happy Birthday Tom!" Suddenly Raoul sprang forth from the throng and threw a large handful of confetti into the air directly over Wyatt, most of which landed in his hair and on his shoulders. As the raucous applause continued, Wyatt stood dumbfounded, with his mouth slightly open and his face growing very red.

Wyatt's eyes darted all throughout the room - quickly absorbing this strange and sudden sight - until they landed on Sean, who along with Rob, Colby and Ping, was standing along the wall directly behind Anjelica. Sean, who was wearing a cone-shaped party hat and tuxedo like most every other gentleman in the room, smiled at Wyatt with a smirk of satisfaction. Sean then raised the glass of wine that he was holding, nodded at Wyatt, and continued to stare intently at the confused detective.

"I don't understand," Morgan said, as the applause began to fade. "What's going on?"

"Well isn't it obvious?" answered Anjelica, "It's a birthday party for one of my nearest and dearest friends, Detective Tom Wyatt." The guests clapped again as Anjelica moved beside Wyatt, sliding her hand under his arm as he stood there in disbelief. "His actual birthday was a few weeks ago but we missed it, so we decided to throw one for him tonight instead."

"You brought us here for this?" Morgan angrily asked Wyatt. "For your birthday party?"

"No, I - uh," stammered Wyatt as he stumbled over his words. "It's not what it looks like. I don't even know these people!"

"Oh, that's our Tom," continued Anjelica, prompting another round of laughter from her guests. "His need for attention is rivaled only by his active imagination. So precious!"

Anjelica kissed Wyatt, leaving a bright red lipstick mark on his cheek for all to see. Morgan, who appeared very angry and agitated, lowered her microphone to her side and approached the detective.

"I hope you're happy," Morgan said angrily. "This little publicity stunt of yours might have just cost me my career. Mark my words that if it does, I'll see to it that it costs you your career too!"

The young reporter then turned away, flipping back her hair as she went storming out of the room with her cameraman scurrying quickly behind her. Rob then stepped forward holding two glasses of wine in his hands. He handed one of them to Anjelica, and then offered the other glass to Wyatt. Wyatt furrowed his brow, gritted his teeth, and began to leave the room with Abby following closely behind him. Rob shrugged his shoulders and took a drink from the glass of wine that he was left holding.

"Oh, and Tom, before you go," Anjelica said, as the detectives stopped and turned toward her, "I'd like to report some missing property. It seems that one of my guests had her cell phone stolen a few days ago." Anjelica then fixed her eyes squarely on Abby. "And ironically enough, based on her description, the thief looked a lot like you."

Abby looked apprehensively at Tom, and then looked back at Anjelica. The detectives looked at each other, and then slipped quickly out of the house. As they exited, Samson appeared in the foyer and closed the front door behind them. The music began again and the guests could be heard cheering. Wyatt and Abby strode quickly down the driveway, doing their best to avoid the two remaining reporters that were waiting to speak to them.

"No comment," barked Wyatt as he and Abby breezed past the journalists, disappearing into the darkness where Wyatt's car was parked.

"What the hell just happened in there?" Abby asked, as she rushed into the passenger seat of Wyatt's car and closed the door.

"I'll tell you what just happened," Wyatt replied, as he jumped in the car and pulled away quickly from the scene. "I just got played."

Back inside, the living room was alive with spirited conversations. The guests continued to blow into their noise-makers, and playfully pull on each other's hats. Sean kicked away a red balloon that had fallen in front of him as he walked up to Anjelica and Rob.

"Well I'd say that couldn't have gone any better," volunteered Rob, as both Colby and Ping approached the group.

"Did I miss something?" Ping asked innocently. "Why did the guest of honor just leave his own birthday party?"

"Well, you see Ping, it's like this," answered Colby, as he placed his hand on Ping's shoulder. "This wasn't really a birthday party. That guy was a cop, and he was coming here to bust us."

"We set a trap," added Rob, "and Sean was the bait."

"I suppose that's one way of putting it," Sean said.

"I still don't understand," said Ping, as he looked at both men confusedly.

"I'll be happy to explain," interjected Anjelica, after taking a quick sip of wine. "A few days ago, Detective Wyatt told Sean that he knew about Blue Shirts, and that he intended to bring everyone involved with the company to justice. Wyatt asked Sean to help him in this little endeavor, but rather than helping him, Sean told me about it."

"After Anjelica found out," Rob continued, "she did some checking up on Wyatt at the police department. She found out that he was a real egomaniac."

"Like most men that I know," Anjelica added, drawing groans from Rob and Colby.

"Anyway," Rob said while pulling a cigar from his jacket pocket, "she also found out that his birthday was last month, and that's when she came up with this plan - which was a stroke of genius, mind you. She had Sean call Wyatt and tell him about an important book that she keeps in her safe - a book that would be the key piece of evidence in his case against Blue Shirts.

"I knew that his ego would get the best of him," Anjelica mentioned, "and that shaming us was more important to him than arresting us. I told Sean to tell him that he could have the book, provided he come to retrieve it on any other night besides tonight. I knew full well that he couldn't resist coming this evening, so that's when I arranged for this impromptu party in his honor."

"So where's the real book?" Ping asked.

"You don't need to worry about that," Anjelica answered. "It's hidden away safely. I removed it from the safe earlier today and had Sean put another book in its place."

"It was a notebook, and all of the pages are blank," volunteered Rob. "That was Anjelica's idea. It was her way of telling Wyatt that he had absolutely nothing on her - or on us. The card was Sean's idea, however," he added, as she turned to Sean. "That was a nice touch."

"So you embarrassed him instead?" Ping asked. "What if that just makes him mad? What if he comes back?"

"He won't be back," Anjelica answered. "The public now believes that he and I are friends, which is a definite conflict of interest as far as the department is concerned. If the police want to pursue this any further, they'll take him off the case, especially after his disastrous appearance on tonight's 11 o'clock news. More importantly, Wyatt doesn't have any evidence on us - absolutely nothing - therefore he has no case."

"So if you're wondering if we're untouchable," Rob added smugly, as he lit his cigar, "stop wondering - because we are."

"We're going to lay low for a few days," Anjelica said, "maybe a week or two, just to be safe. After that, it will be back to business as usual. Is that clear?"

Anjelica smiled as she stared at the men gathered around her, all of whom nodded in agreement as they raised their glasses and nodded at her in agreement. As he took a drink of wine, Sean walked slowly through the center of the room, where Avery was standing with a pouty look on her face.

"I'm ready to dance," slurred Avery, clumsily holding a glass full of bourbon and crushed ice. "Will you dance with me?"

"Of course," Sean replied, as he took her hand into his and slipped his arm behind her waist. As the music slowed, Sean pulled her closer as the music grew softer. Avery burrowed her face into his shoulder, and Sean closed his eyes as he held her tightly. He breathed a sigh of relief, happy that the evening was ending. He was content.

A few days later, Rob, Colby and Ping found themselves sitting on the steps of Sean's front porch. It was warm, and the evening sun was beginning to set. Sean walked through the front door wearing a white apron and holding a large plate full of hamburgers and hot dogs.

"Dinner is served," Sean said, as the men came up and grabbed some food from the plate.

"Man, there's nothing like the taste of charcoal," announced Colby, as he snatched a burger from the plate, placed it on a bun and took a large bite. "I just can't do gas grills, you know? The taste just isn't the same."

"Ah, don't mention it," replied Sean. "I'm just glad that it's finally warm enough to start grilling out."

"If I keep eating like this," Ping said, as he took a bite of a hot dog and patted his belly, "I'll need to go on a diet. Or buy larger clothes."

"So no kid tonight?" asked Rob, as he squeezed some ketchup onto his hamburger bun.

"No, he's with his mom," answered Sean, who sat down on the porch steps between Colby and Ping.

"So how's that going?" Rob asked. "Are you guys still getting along?"

"For the most part," Sean replied. "She's happy, Braden's happy. I'm happy too."

"And how's your dad?" Rob inquired.

"Better," answered Sean. "He's not out of the woods by any stretch, but his health is improving. The next few weeks will definitely tell us a lot. He has a few more tests, a few more things that the doctors have to check out. We'll see."

"That's good to hear," Rob said, as he took a bite of his hamburger. "Make sure he takes it easy. It's important that he doesn't try to do too much. Make sure he doesn't rush things."

"Speaking of time, when do you think we'll hear from Anjelica again?" asked Colby, as he twisted off the cap of his bottle of beer. "It's been two weeks. I'm beginning to wonder."

"She's just lying low right now," Rob said. "She received a lot of attention for that stunt she pulled at the house. Give it some time."

"So has anybody heard what happened to that detective?" Ping asked.

"Our good buddy Wyatt?" answered Colby in his familiar twang. "Last week I couldn't turn on the damn TV without seeing his face. He got suspended or something."

"He was placed on administrative leave," Rob added, "He's being investigated for police misconduct. They'll probably get him on a few charges, like obstruction of justice or tampering with evidence. He'll retire before they complete the investigation, especially with him being the age that he is. Either way, he's through here. He's ancient history."

The men finished their meals and watched the sun disappear into the horizon. For a few seconds, it was quiet - there was no conversation, and the only noise that could be heard was the sound of a neighbor's lawn mower in the distance.

The mower's engine turned off, and Sean stood up and began walking toward his front door when a familiar alert sounded on his cell phone. Within seconds, Rob's phone, then Colby's and Ping's, sounded the same alert. They all reached for their phones and examined them, swiping the screens deliberately yet frantically at the same time. They put their plates down on the porch steps and smiled at each other.

"Time to go to work," Sean said, as he looked at his friends and then peered off into the distance at the remaining fragments of sunlight that were left in the sky. One by one, the men stood up and began filtering into Sean's house. After his friends were all inside, Sean lingered for a moment on the porch, and watched as the sun finally disappeared on the horizon. Once it was gone, he rose to his feet and made his way through the doorway, joining his friends in the kitchen. It felt good to be home.

Special Thanks

Kevin Kifer

Scott Hall

Scott McBrayer

David Sloan

Kenny Rice

Han Fan

John McDaniel

Maria E.

Kimberly Leslie

Brad Elswick

Nathan Benge

Annie Gallina

Wade Smith

Rick Roberts

Misty Roberts

Stacey Gillespie

Conner Crisp

Marge Crisp

Cindy McCain

Angie Davis

Blue Shirts

written by

Michael Crisp

MICHAEL CRISP'S OTHER BOOKS INCLUDE:

The Kentucky Bucket List: 100 Ways to Have a Real Kentucky Experience

The Tennessee Bucket List: 100 Ways to Have a Real Tennessee Experience

The Ohio Bucket List: 100 Ways to Have a Real Ohio Experience

Murder in the Mountains: The Muriel Baldridge Story

The Making of The Very Worst Thing

AS A DIRECTOR, MICHAEL CRISP'S FILMS INCLUDE:

The Very Worst Thing

When Happy Met Froggie

Legendary: When Baseball Came to the Bluegrass

A Cut Above: The Legend of Larry Roberts

A Life of Its Own

The Death of Floyd Collins

Available at Local Bookstores and Online at Amazon.com